Anything y...
be held...

Jessica wept as the... wrists. She couldn't believe that the handsome ship's captain was actually accusing her of being a thief. "I didn't take anything!" she yelled. "Somebody get my sister. I didn't take that ring!"

"I'm sorry, Ms. Wakefield," the captain barked. "You're spending the night in jail."

As the Juma police officers led her down the gangplank, a single ray of hope penetrated Jessica's gloomy thoughts.

She was in trouble again, big trouble, which meant that her guardian angel might appear and swoop her off to safety. In the last few weeks, her loving mystery man had saved her life at least three times. Would he help her now?

Jessica turned her head, searching the shadows in vain. No one came to her rescue.

Bantam Books in the Sweet Valley University series:

SWEET VALLEY UNIVERSITY ™

SS Heartbreak

Written by
Laurie John

Created by
FRANCINE PASCAL

BANTAM BOOKS
NEW YORK · TORONTO · LONDON · SYDNEY · AUCKLAND

SS HEARTBREAK
A BANTAM BOOK : 0 553 50347 2

Originally published in USA by Bantam Books

First publication in Great Britain

PRINTING HISTORY
Bantam edition published 1996

Conceived by Francine Pascal

Produced by Daniel Weiss Associates, Inc,
33 West 17th Street, New York, NY 10011

Bantam Books are published by Transworld Publishers Ltd,
61–63 Uxbridge Road, London W5 5SA,
in Australia by Transworld Publishers (Australia) Pty Ltd,
15–25 Helles Avenue, Moorebank, NSW 2170,
and in New Zealand by Transworld Publishers (NZ) Ltd,
3 William Pickering Drive, Albany, Auckland.

Printed and bound in Great Britain by
Cox & Wyman Ltd, Reading, Berkshire.

To Nicole Pascal Johansson

Chapter One

Isabella Ricci was so mad, her cool gray eyes were smoking. She jabbed a perfectly manicured finger against Danny Wyatt's chest. "Why can't you mind your own business?" she asked for what seemed like the millionth time. She winced as Danny shot her a contemptuous look.

"There it is in a nutshell," he said. He slowly shook his handsome dark head. "Everything that's wrong with our culture. Mind your own business. Look the other way. Don't get involved. Well, that may be the easy solution, but it's not the ethical one. The guy has a right to know."

If Isabella heard the word *ethical* one more time, she thought she might scream. Usually she admired Danny's strong sense of values. Part of what had attracted her to him in the first place was that he didn't just talk about doing the right thing—he actually tried to do it.

But now he was about to commit an act that was as wrong as could be, at least according to Isabella's code. He was being unbearably self-righteous about it, too.

Isabella couldn't believe that she was actually sitting in a cabin on the SS *Homecoming Queen*, fighting with her boyfriend. Arguing was the last thing she'd expected to happen between her and Danny during the week-long cruise.

The SS *Homecoming Queen* was fitted out with every imaginable indulgence and diversion, from espresso bar to rifle range. And all the passengers were college students. The only adults in sight were gorgeously weathered Captain Avedon and his uniformed crew.

But instead of living out their tropical fantasies, Isabella and Danny, along with most of the others in their group, had hit emotionally rough waters. Right now Isabella could cheerfully have tossed Danny overboard. And thrown his ethics in after him.

Isabella thought back to a couple of weeks earlier, when Danny had received a letter from Jason Pierce, his best friend from high school. Jason had written to say that he was getting married on the *Homecoming Queen*, and he wanted Danny to be his best man. Danny was dying to hang out with Jason again and to meet the woman he was going to marry, but Danny hadn't been able to afford the spring break cruise in the Caribbean.

Just as Danny had been ready to call Jason and tell him he wouldn't be in the wedding, Elizabeth Wakefield had given Danny—and the rest of her friends—a huge surprise.

Having inherited a small fortune from William White, the criminally insane Sweet Valley University student who'd stalked her for several months, she'd decided to use some of his money to buy pleasure for herself and some of her friends whom he'd terrorized.

Isabella had been thrilled about the romantic prospects for herself and Danny. And the trip had promised to be a special time for other couples as well.

But now she and Danny were arguing because Danny and Elizabeth had caught Tom Watts kissing Jason's fiancée, Nicole Riley. Tom wasn't only Danny's best friend and roommate, he was also Elizabeth's boyfriend.

In Isabella's opinion, it was bad enough that famously nonviolent Danny had reacted to the kiss by punching Tom. Now he seemed determined to make the situation even worse. He was convinced that it was his duty as an ethical man to tell Jason what he had seen.

What Danny saw as ethical, Isabella saw as hysterical. And interfering. And destructive. And just

3

plain stupid. Isabella was determined to straighten him out before he went charging in like Napoleon, wrecking people's lives. One kiss. One fully clothed, fresh-air kiss. Hardly the end of the world.

Even if Tom and Nicole had been caught in a truly compromising position, who had elected Danny Wyatt High Commissioner of Morals? As far as Isabella was concerned, Danny should stay out of the entire situation. This was male bonding at its worst.

Isabella hadn't a shred of doubt that Jason would respond with some dopey manly gesture of his own. Since Danny had already punched out Tom for him, he'd have to go him one better. He might call off the wedding, for instance. Isabella could almost see Nicole's stricken face as Jason canceled their rosy future. Over one kiss.

"What do you care if you mess up a couple of people's lives and everybody's vacation? I swear, I'll never speak to you again if you do it," she said to Danny.

"I say the guy has a right to know," Danny repeated. "What kind of wife is Nicole going to be if she's kissing some other guy less than a week before the wedding?"

"What kind of guy hits his best friend without asking any questions?" Isabella countered. "I still can't believe you swung."

Danny looked down at his bruised knuckles. "I can't quite believe it either," he admitted. "It was just some kind of instinctual move," he went on. "The way Elizabeth flipped out, I had to do something. And I guess I'm taking my role as Jason's best man pretty seriously."

"A little too seriously, if you ask me," Isabella said. She glanced around the cabin that Danny was sharing with Tom. Even with its bunk beds and nautical motif, it bore a striking resemblance to the room the two guys shared at SVU—enough books and magazines to stock a small library, a portable backgammon set, Danny's free weights, and Tom's crumpled clothes. Tom's crumpled everything, as a matter of fact. He was as messy as Danny was neat. In fact, Tom and Danny were different in lots of ways. But until an hour ago, Isabella had thought nothing could come between them.

"Oh, I get it," Danny said suddenly. Holding his head in his hands, he sank down onto the bottom bunk. "How could I have been so blind?"

For a moment Isabella thought he'd come to his senses. But only for a moment. "I guess it's pretty easy for you to imagine being in Nicole's shoes." Danny's mouth tightened grimly. "Up there on the deck, with the moon shining down, what woman could possibly have resisted Tom Watts?" He looked her straight in the eyes, the

5

way he always did. But there was none of the usual melting warmth in his gaze.

"Could you have said no to Tom, Isabella?"

It's a good thing I'm honest, Jessica Wakefield thought as she let herself into the cabin next to Danny and Tom's. The door was the fourth she'd managed to open with one of the many keys to her many pieces of luggage. *If I were a thief, my pockets would be ripping by now.* In the course of her explorations she'd found two solid gold watches, a cigarette lighter that played "Smoke Gets in Your Eyes," and a pair of diamond cuff links.

But she wasn't looking for jewelry. Or passports, or condoms, or socks with holes in the toes, or any of the other things she'd come across so far. She was looking for a button. More precisely, she was looking for the place where a button had been. A plain and simple, everyday, ordinary American shirt button. Jessica looked down at the small round object. It was off white, the color of a vanilla milk shake, with a pearly finish. It had four tiny holes in it, and each one had frayed white thread running through it. If she had to estimate its diameter, she would guess maybe half an inch.

Of all the things she'd ever obsessed over, this had to be the stupidest. The button belonged to the shirt of the mystery man who'd been hovering

6

behind her for weeks, almost like a guardian angel. He always managed to show up when she was in danger. Most recently he'd jumped into the ocean and saved her from drowning when she'd fallen overboard.

Unfortunately he'd disappeared before she could say thank you. The only clue Jessica had to his identity was the button she had found clenched inside her fist when she'd regained consciousness on the deck of the ship. Now she had to find a shirt with identical buttons—and one button missing. So she was methodically working her way through the guys' cabins. She'd looked in laundry bags. She'd looked on shower rods. She'd looked in drawers.

As she opened a drawer inside the cabin next to Danny and Tom's, a terrible thought occurred to her. What if some well-meaning person working in the laundry had replaced the missing button? Some well-meaning jerk who didn't realize what its absence meant to Jessica Wakefield?

Suddenly the voices in the next cabin caught her attention. It wasn't that she was eavesdropping. She would no sooner spy on someone's conversation than . . . rifle through someone's drawers uninvited. Unless, of course, the conversation happened to concern a person whose well-being was almost as important to her as her own—her identical twin sister, Elizabeth.

7

And any conversation that concerned Tom Watts definitely concerned Elizabeth. *So technically I'm not eavesdropping. I'm just looking out for Elizabeth,* Jessica thought.

She caught sight of herself in the mirror over the dresser. Was there a hint of guilt in her blue-green eyes? If so, it must have been because she wasn't listening hard enough. Then, as Isabella and Danny's voices grew more heated, she distinctly heard the words *Tom, Nicole,* and *kissing* in the same sentence.

Dropping all pretense, Jessica glued her ear to the wall.

Chapter Two

Isabella didn't know whether the roaring she heard in her ears was the pounding of waves against the ship or the pulsing of her own blood. How dare Danny accuse her of having romantic feelings for Tom?

"Of all the despicable things I've ever heard, that has to be the worst." Her voice rose with emotion. "Don't you remember the night we found Tom after he'd been attacked last semester? And you told me how much it helped you to be with a girl who cared about Tom as much as you did?"

Her eyes threatened to fill with tears as she remembered that bittersweet time. William White's racism and obsession with Elizabeth might have cost Tom's life. In fact, all the SVU students now safely aboard the *Homecoming Queen* would have died if William's desperate plot to possess Elizabeth had succeeded.

But out of William's evil some good had sprung. After sharing a near death experience, the SVU gang had been drawn together. Now the group shared a bond that they had thought would last a lifetime. Unfortunately over the last couple of days there had been a lot of arguing and misunderstanding on the luxury cruise ship.

Isabella folded her arms across her chest and glared at her boyfriend. "I can't believe you're turning it all around this way!"

"I'm turning things around?"

"You bet you are!" she yelled.

Something in Danny seemed to soften, and he dropped his gaze. Following his eyes, she noticed that he was wearing a pair of cross-training sneakers that looked as though they'd lived through several Olympics. Most of the other SVU kids, Isabella included, had bought a whole new wardrobe for their spring break vacation. But Danny had just managed to scrape together the rental fees for the tuxedo he needed as Jason's best man.

The sight of those battered shoes made Isabella groan inwardly. Was Danny feeling insecure? Maybe that was what this fight was really about. Maybe the sight of Nicole kissing Tom had made Danny doubt the security of his relationship with Isabella. Was it back to square one for them?

"I care about Tom," Isabella repeated, but in a gentler voice. "But there's only one guy I'm in love with."

"There was a time—" Danny began insistently.

Isabella sat down next to him. "Yes, there was a time when I was interested in Tom," she agreed. "But I thought we'd resolved this, Danny. It's supposed to make you feel fabulous—positively fabuloso—that the divine Isabella Ricci, who could have any man on campus, chose you."

"Any man on campus?" Danny raised his head and offered her something that looked almost like a smile. "I thought it was any man in America," he added.

Isabella reached out and took Danny's hand. "Any man in the world."

"And she picked me. The goddess picked me." Now Danny gave her a full-scale grin. "There must be something wrong with her."

"Must be." She pretended to consider. "Maybe it's . . . hmmm . . . her hopeless addiction to backgammon."

She reached for the board, propped it on her knees, and began to set up her pieces.

As usual Isabella took the dark brown pieces, leaving the off-white ones for Danny—it was one of their private jokes about the difference in their skin tones.

Isabella watched as Danny grasped the backgammon pieces. She loved looking at his strong hands. In fact, she usually loved everything about him. If she could just get him to rethink his definition of right and wrong, they could quit debating someone else's relationship problems. Then the rest of the cruise would be pure pleasure.

"But seriously," she said as they each rolled out a single die to determine the first move. "You've come to your senses, right? You're not going to say word one to Jason." It was a statement, not a question.

Danny won the roll with his six to Isabella's four. "I guess there's no doubt about the right move to make," he said as he picked up two pieces and moved them across the board. "And that's no move."

"Thank you." She sighed with relief and rattled the dice in her cup. She rolled a six and a five, and completed her turn.

"I'll keep my mouth shut," Danny continued. "But no way are Tom Watts and I friends anymore." He gave his dice a ferocious shake.

Isabella looked at the set of Danny's jaw. She

12

knew she'd pushed him as far as he would go. Now was not the time to persuade him that he shouldn't shun Tom just because he made one mistake. "Have it your way," she said, shrugging.

But inside she vowed that not only would a wedding still take place on this cruise—an important friendship would be saved as well.

Jessica looked up in surprise from the drawer she was searching. The news she'd inadvertently heard from the cabin next door was startling, to say the least. But now she understood why Elizabeth was looking so upset.

Jessica wasn't the most dedicated member of the Tom Watts fan club. The guy was about as exciting as a stale Girl Scout cookie. But Tom had been a good friend to Jessica in recent months. And she had to admit that he had a great way of making Elizabeth happy.

Jessica and Elizabeth might reflect each other physically, with their long blond hair and slim figures, but it was Tom who mirrored Elizabeth's interest in journalism and academics. And the couple of times when Jessica had walked in on them unexpectedly, the air around the couple had really being sizzling.

Well, one thing was clear from the debate raging next door. Tom and Nicole hadn't been discussing international disarmament when Elizabeth and Danny had surprised them on the deck. It sounded more like they were making their own nuclear fission.

After halfheartedly looking through a stack of plaid boxer shorts, Jessica closed the dresser drawer with an impatient shove. She could cross off this cabin as far as her mystery man was concerned.

Jessica tucked the button deep into one of the pockets of her tight white jeans. She should quit searching for clues about the guardian angel who'd been watching over her and find Elizabeth. Her twin was probably in need of some major comfort.

Jessica sighed. Maybe solitude loved company, but somehow she really didn't want Elizabeth and Tom to break up. She was used to the Elizabeth-and-Tom thing, and it would be kind of nice if something in life stayed the same for more than two minutes in a row.

Besides, Elizabeth was her sister. At times she was a sermonizing killjoy, and she did have an annoying tendency to keep her side of their room as clean as a doctor's office. But their twin bond gave them a kind of closeness that was almost supernatural. For instance, Elizabeth had actually looked worse than Jessica had felt after Jessica's near drowning last night.

But if Jessica allowed herself to think about the night before, she'd start obsessing about her mystery man again, and she didn't have time for that.

For once, it was Elizabeth who needed her sister's help. And Jessica wasn't about to let her down..

Elizabeth sat hunched in misery, her face resting on her clenched fists, her elbows digging into her thighs. "No," she groaned repeatedly as the unbearable image flashed again and again in her mind.

As hard as she tried to push the picture away, her mental movie projector refused to switch off or play a different scene. It was as if the sight of Nicole and Tom embracing had burned itself into Elizabeth's brain. *Embracing*—the word was a euphemism for what Tom and Nicole had been doing. Embracing was what parents did. Tom and Nicole had been entwined. Enmeshed.

Their arms had been wound tightly around each other, and their lips had looked as if they'd been glued together. Even if she traveled to the ends of the earth, Elizabeth wouldn't be able to escape the image. As long as she lived, that kiss would live in her mind, tormenting her.

The idea of Tom kissing another woman seemed so impossible that Elizabeth could barely process the information. It was something she wouldn't have expected to see in a million years.

Tom and Elizabeth had never even discussed the concept of fidelity. They hadn't needed to. They'd talked about nearly everything under the sun, but on a few essential issues they'd so clearly been as one that silence had said enough.

Their kisses had said enough.

In the fall, before she'd started dating Tom, William White had tricked Elizabeth into having scary suspicions about the elusive Tom Watts. She'd even thought—briefly—that Tom was the leader of a secret society that was responsible for racist attacks on campus, among other horrors. But Elizabeth had quickly come to her senses. It was William who had been the true villain. And as she and Tom had worked together to expose him on the campus TV station, they'd developed a rock-hard faith in each other.

Their romance had been built on that solid foundation. And unlike many of the relationships around them, theirs was about more than physical attraction—a lot more. Above all else, Tom Watts and Elizabeth Wakefield were about trust.

At least, they used to be about trust. Until the

Rock of Gibraltar had turned out to be made of clay.

Once again she saw Tom and Nicole's kiss in the theater of her mind. Suddenly the melody of "Our Love Is Here to Stay" began to play in Elizabeth's head. It was a song she and Tom often hummed together. Now she'd never be able to listen to that song again—not without bursting into tears.

There were a million things she wouldn't be able to do without crying. She probably wouldn't even be able to get up in the morning without drying her first tears of the day. There were just so many things that had somehow been better because of Tom. Now everything she saw would be a ghostly reminder of a dead past.

I still love you, Tom, Elizabeth silently cried. *Even though I hate you, I love you.* For a moment she clung to the exquisite pain of her loss. Then something inside her rebelled.

What right did she have to turn her boyfriend's cheating into the tragedy of the century? So another college romance had gone down the tubes—big deal. It was hardly as important as an earthquake or children starving in Africa. *Who needs men, anyway?* she asked herself.

Elizabeth stood up, narrowly missing the top bunk, and stared at herself in the mirror. Pushing back her silky blond hair, rubbing off her lip gloss with one hand, she made a vow. Not only was she through with Tom, she was through with romance. As soon as she got back home, she was going to dedicate her life to something that really mattered.

Maybe she'd try to line up a summer job with her congressman and really learn about the political process. Better yet, she'd join the Peace Corps. Why throw her energies away on shallow, faithless college men when there were suffering souls who needed her?

Elizabeth's heart swelled as she envisioned herself gliding through the crowded wards of some far-off ramshackle hospital. Then she dreamed of the day when Tom would pick up his morning paper and see that she'd won the Nobel Prize—on that day he'd finally understand the magnitude of his mistake. "Elizabeth," he would whisper as Nicole or her successor looked on through a mist of tears.

Elizabeth sank back onto the narrow bed. The only problem with her vision was that she wasn't remotely interested in being a saint. She was a normal, healthy eighteen-year-old, and she'd truly been in love, and she was totally and absolutely crushed.

A softly urgent knocking at the door drew her out of her reverie. Then Elizabeth stiffened, and her stomach flipped over.

She would know that knock anywhere. If an orchestra were playing Beethoven's Fifth and sirens were blaring in her ears, she would still be able to distinguish the sound of Tom Watts knocking on a door.

Usually it was her favorite sound in the world. Now she felt fresh tears threatening to spill over onto her cheeks.

"Go away," she said tersely.

"Elizabeth—"

Even through the thick wood, she could hear the layers of emotion in his voice.

"Please, you have to talk to me. I love—"

The intimate word made her feel even worse. "Don't bother claiming you love me. Just leave me alone!"

"Elizabeth, please, I'm begging you, let me—"

"Let you what?" she shouted. "Tell me I was hallucinating? Tell me it didn't matter? It was just one tiny little kiss in the great big scheme of things?"

As she wrote Tom's script for him Elizabeth forced herself to stop the flow of tears. She wasn't going to give him the satisfaction. No way. She swallowed hard and drew a steadying breath.

Elizabeth stood and crossed the small room so she could stand next to the door. "You have a

19

great gift for words, Tom. But I'm afraid this is one situation you can't talk away. So don't even try," she said softly.

"Please, Liz—" he started again.

Willing perfect coldness into her features, she flung open the door and looked straight into his eyes—which were red rimmed and swollen.

Welcome to the club, she thought bitterly.

"Elizabeth," he said, his voice breaking over the syllables. "Give me a chance to make it up to you."

She shook her head. "I don't want to hear it. Any of it. The only sound I want to hear out of you ever again is your footsteps—heading in the opposite direction."

He just stood there, mutely beseeching her.

For a brief moment she felt a treacherous urge to console him, as if he'd been the one betrayed. In a flash she realized how empty life would be without Tom Watts's kisses in it. Before she could act on her feelings, she slammed the door with all her might.

Now maybe both of them would get the point. *It's over.*

Sometimes it's hard to believe we're only minutes apart in age, Jessica thought as she looked at Elizabeth's stricken face.

Jessica hadn't seen so much anxiety over a measly kiss since she was thirteen years old and playing spin the bottle. Elizabeth might be the one who got put into advanced-placement English and history classes, but when it came to experience with men, Jessica was light-years older than her sister.

At eighteen Jessica Wakefield had the dubious honor of being the former Mrs. Michael McAllery. The marriage had been a series of disasters, culminating in a nightmare accidental shooting between Mike and the twins' older brother, Steven. From his hospital bed Mike had been decent enough to offer an annulment. But Jessica would never forget their time together.

With a passionate, if short-lived, marriage in her past, Jessica looked at everyone else's romantic relationships through a different kind of filter. When she thought back to the intimacy she and Mike had shared, a single kiss, even a steamy one, seemed fairly insignificant.

She put an arm around her sister's shoulders. "Come on, Liz. You know what the song says—a kiss is just a kiss."

Then, out of nowhere, the memory of Mike's alleged womanizing worked itself into her brain. Not only had he often come home reeking of beer, his hair had frequently smelled of other women's perfume. If she'd ever actually seen him

21

in someone else's arms, she probably would have died of the pain.

Jessica shook her head vigorously, trying to clear it. Maybe Elizabeth wasn't overreacting after all. Maybe a kiss wasn't just a kiss, any more than a chocolate chip cookie was just a cookie when you were on a diet. It was the chink in the armor, the beginning of the end.

She gave Liz another squeeze. "That no-good, slimy cheat. Forget about him."

The forlorn daze on Elizabeth's face gave way to sisterly amusement. "Aren't you the one who said 'a kiss is just a kiss' a second ago?" she asked. "And everyone gets that line wrong. It's 'a kiss is *still* a kiss.'"

"Whatever," Jessica said impatiently. She hated it when Elizabeth got hung up on details. "We can't give men an inch, that's the point." She paused to consider. "Of course—"

"What, Jess?"

"Well, I was thinking—"

"You, thinking? Now there's a novel idea."

"I do think now and then," Jessica announced huffily. "You didn't get all the brain cells."

Elizabeth sighed deeply. "Brain cells? Me? Are you kidding? Where were they the day I fell in love with Tom?"

"Where were they the day we fell in love with whoever?" Jessica said, shrugging. Then the image of the mystery man came sailing into her mind. "Anyway, here's what I was thinking, Liz," she said, perking up. "Isn't there anybody you could have kissed? Without feeling as though you were being unfaithful to Tom?"

"Absolutely not!" Elizabeth replied indignantly.

"Are you sure? I mean, what if you'd been up there on the deck feeling depressed about something and Todd had come along? With the moon shimmering on the waves and everything. Are you positive you wouldn't have succumbed?" She raised an eyebrow. "You wouldn't let him give you one little kiss?" She did her best to make it sound like only half a chocolate chip cookie—and from someone else's plate, so the calories really didn't count.

Elizabeth sat up straight. "Jessica, what is this, the third degree? Of course I wouldn't kiss Todd. Or anyone else. At least I wouldn't have before tonight," she added, making her meaning perfectly clear.

"Well, I wouldn't kiss Todd either," Jessica had to agree. But as for her mystery man—that was another story. She hoped she didn't have to have another near-death experience before she felt his strong arms around her.

Closing her eyes, she drifted into a dream state. Was he the one? The man who would love her forever, to the end of time? "Until death do us part . . ." she heard as organ music swelled in the background.

Abruptly Jessica remembered her promise to herself and her parents. She would get all the way through college before she even considered marrying again. Studying and having harmless fun—that's what her life was about.

The thought of marriage reminded her of Jason and Nicole. As her focus widened to take in the cabin, her gaze lingered on the gleaming bird's-eye maple of the sliding closet doors. Half open, they revealed an array of spaghetti-strap sundresses, backless evening gowns, and the alluring red silk dress that she'd planned to wear to the wedding.

"Nicole and Jason!" she exclaimed.

"What about them?" Elizabeth asked in a bitter voice.

"The wedding! I was totally psyched to go to the wedding. You're not going to say anything to Jason, are you, Liz?"

Elizabeth's mouth tightened the way it did when she was about to take one of her principled stands.

But after a few moments Elizabeth shook her head. "The less I have to do with the two of them, the better," she said, her voice ragged. "There's only one relationship I'm concerned with—mine and Tom's." Her shoulders rose and fell wearily. "It's over, Jess. Tom Watts is the past tense. And now, if you don't mind, I'd like to turn out the lights and cry myself to sleep."

La Contessa di Mondicci was the perfect picture of shipboard indolence. Right now no one was looking at the picture, but she didn't mind at all.

After the shocking events of the night before, she needed some solitude before she could face her friends—or anyone else. The former Lila Fowler considered herself a classic Californian, but definitely not of the let-it-all-hang-out variety. Fainting on the deck was enough public display of emotion to last her a lifetime.

Not that anyone would blame me, she thought grimly. Lila closed her eyes, remembering the scene as a helicopter had made a roaring descent onto the *Homecoming Queen,* like some mythic bird descending from the heavens. A dark, handsome man had stepped out.

As he approached the curious crowd who had

gathered on the deck, an insane shrieking filled Lila's head. The most impossible thing in all of history was happening before her eyes. Tisiano was alive!

The ecstasy and terror of the situation had been too much for her. She'd fainted into Bruce's arms. Minutes later Lila had awakened to discover that the man was Tisiano's brother. Leonardo di Mondicci was the globe-trotting owner of a modeling agency and one member of Tisiano's family whom Lila had never met.

Leonardo had gently helped Lila to her feet, then announced that he had papers for her to sign. But she'd been in no shape last night to sign anything, especially important documents affecting her financial future. So she and Leonardo were to talk at noon in the Venetian Lounge.

Part of the reason she wanted to lie on a deck chair and do nothing but soak up the late-morning sun was that it was going to take all her strength to cope with Leonardo. He'd been nice enough last night, and very apologetic for the shock he had caused—but it had been instantly apparent that he didn't quite approve of her.

As Lila stretched out on a reclining deck chair, a woven cotton blanket tucked around her bikini-clad form, she tuned in to the restorative power of the elements. Lulled by the rhythmic swelling of the sea beneath her, she pushed aside her worries and sighed with pleasure as the hot Caribbean sun and the cool salty breeze competed for control of her personal climate.

A feeling of gratitude swept over her. Really, there was nothing like a cruise to heal body and soul. The SS *Homecoming Queen* might have been a notch down from the yacht on which she and Tisiano had sailed the Mediterranean, as guests of a Greek shipbuilder, but it wasn't exactly shabby.

Of course, it helped that the crew had instantly recognized her as more than just another rich college student. She didn't need to proffer the calling card engraved with the Mondicci family crest in order to get special attention. Even those who had no idea she was an Italian countess by marriage seemed to recognize that she was a California princess by birth.

Lila felt a shadow fall over her, and she opened her eyes. Shading her face with one hand, she looked up to see a steward hovering attentively at her side, a cup of chamomile tea on the tray he was holding.

"*Grazie,*" she murmured as she took the cup. "Thank you," she amended, remembering that the crew members probably weren't Italian.

She sipped the sweetly aromatic tea, then set it down on the deck as a pleasant drowsiness reclaimed her. Even holding a cup required more effort than she wanted to exert at the moment.

Somehow she needed all her energy just to be. At the same time, existence itself seemed like all that was necessary.

She'd let her friends fill up the hours with shuffleboard, backgammon, miniature golf, and assorted aerobic activities. She could hear their far-off laughter, and it didn't lure her.

Having witnessed the tragic death of her husband, the dashing Count Tisiano di Mondicci, and then narrowly survived a mountain crash in Bruce Patman's two-seater Cessna, she was grateful just to be breathing.

She closed her eyes again and sank deeper into relaxation as the sun and soft breeze played against her skin. Falling sleep, she tuned in to the musical beat of the waves.

They seemed to be serenading her in Italian, singing a fifties pop tune that had been special to Tisiano. She could hear his voice in her head. *Quando sei qui con me, questa stanza non a piu paretti*—

Thinking of Tisiano made her feel happy and sad at the same time. She knew that eventually she would have to bury even the memory of him— and Bruce was certainly helping her to do that— but she was pleased that she still had a part of Tisiano inside her. If it had been she who had died a fiery death in an explosion, she wouldn't have wanted him to mourn forever, but she wouldn't have wanted him to forget her in a moment, either.

Lila smiled dreamily, remembering how strong the love between her and Tisiano had been. "When you are here with me, the room no longer has walls . . ." The song's English translation perfectly described their boundless passion.

But then there had been the other days—and nights too—when Lila had been alone. In her heart of hearts, she knew that the marriage might not have gone on forever.

Tisiano had periodically abandoned her, zigzagging Europe to sell the computer parts that had bolstered his considerable family fortune. Being home alone with only servants for company, even in a magnificent palazzo, had grown lonely and boring.

Just before he died, Tisiano had told her he wanted to take her everywhere with him from that point on. But way deep down, had he meant it? Or had he secretly liked things the way they were? He'd had his freedom, as well as Lila, the beautiful princess who pined for him in the palace while he, the brave knight, wrestled with the dragons in the forest.

And would she have enjoyed the twentieth or thirtieth business trip as much as she would have enjoyed the first few? Maybe she would have begun to feel like a piece of baggage—gorgeous, expensive baggage, but baggage nonetheless.

Now she would never know. There hadn't been time to ask all the questions, let alone answer them. Lila and Tisiano hadn't gotten beyond the honeymoon to the reality-testing stage of their marriage. And looking at the marriage from the romantic point of view, maybe she could take some comfort in its tragic brevity.

The more she thought about it, as she drifted dreamily from one notion to the next, the more she saw an eerie aura of beauty surrounding Tisiano's death—and the death of their love. It had come in the midst of pleasure, with a merciful swiftness. Shattering as it had been, it had to have been less painful than a slow disintegration.

Lila's thoughts turned to Bruce, the one man who'd even come near to getting as close to her as Tisiano had. For as long as she'd known him, Bruce had loved to pass himself off as a shallow, arrogant jerk who thought of no one but himself. But the plane crash had left more than physical marks on him. Bruce had revealed to Lila a tender and loving side of himself that few would even believe existed.

Lila's thoughts scattered and her eyes flew open as a deft hand grabbed the blanket that was covering her. Bruce's sleekly handsome face grinned down at her. "Hey, beautiful."

"Give that back!" she squealed, clutching the blanket.

"Not until I get a good look," he said, his blue eyes reflecting adoration.

"I'm freezing!" she protested, hugging herself.

"You're freezing. Yeah, right." Bruce raised his eyebrows. "You survived the mountain snow in a cocktail dress, but you're freezing to death in eighty-degree sunshine."

"You're leaving out the windchill factor," Lila returned severely.

"Ah. In that case—" With a reluctant sigh, Bruce let the blanket flutter down around her.

Perching on the edge of her deck chair, he bent down, dropping small kisses across the bridge of her nose. "You're not burning the most beautiful nose in the world, are you?"

"No, I'm not. Can't you smell all the lotion I'm wearing?" If there was anything Lila had learned as a European wife, it was how to look after her skin. "But what about you?" she asked with concern. She reached up and touched the scar under Bruce's right eyebrow—a souvenir from their nightmare plane crash. "You know what Dr. Jabbour said about the sun and new scar tissue."

Bruce shrugged. "So I can't be a model. Who cares?"

"Are you kidding?" Lila asked. "You could shave your head and tattoo your face and you'd still be model material." She ran a tender finger the length of his wound. "Even so, I'm glad to see how well the scar is healing."

"The power of love," Bruce said solemnly.

He does love me, she thought. *Beneath the banter, he really cares.*

The realization was both thrilling and comforting, but she couldn't resist toying with him. Not that he would want her to resist.

"How powerful is that power?" she said. "Enough to make you get me a cold drink?"

"Cold drink!" he protested. "What happened to the windchill factor?"

"I don't know." Lila shrugged and smiled enticingly. "Something came along and heated up the atmosphere."

"I take that as a compliment, but—" Bruce looked around, his symmetrical features compressing in irritation. "Aren't we paying people to deluge us with anything we want?"

She gave him a playful shove. "Now you sound like a spoiled rich brat."

"Look who's talking," he retorted as she lazily reached for the tube of sunblock.

"Hard work," Lila drawled, stroking the apricot-scented lotion onto her golden forearms. "But someone's got to do it."

"Which means that my job is getting the drinks," Bruce said.

"Exactly. But I'll make it worth your while. I

promise." She yawned hugely. The sunblock dropped to the deck.

Bruce bent to cap the tube. "Plan to make room for two under that blanket when I get back." He kissed her gently on the lips and smoothed her hair.

"I'll be waiting," Lila murmured as she listened to his receding footsteps.

It's over, Alexandra Rollins thought dismally as Noah Pearson looked away from her. The silence between them seemed as vast as the ocean.

It was hard to believe that just weeks ago, she and Noah had spoken for hours and hours at a time. Of course, that had been over the telephone. It had seemed that the world would end before the talk ran out. Now they were having trouble fitting two sentences together.

Was there any hope?

"Brrrrng brrrrng," Alex finally said.

Noah blinked. "Bring?"

"I'm trying to sound like a telephone ringing." Alex knew she sounded cranky, but she couldn't help herself. Suddenly it seemed as though everything had to be explained. "The point I'm trying to make is that maybe we need to have a phone conversation again," she said. "Because we don't seem to be doing too brilliantly face-to-face."

They'd actually met over the phone—sort of.

At first they'd been two anonymous voices at the opposite ends of a campus hot line, Alex desperate to escape from the clutches of alcohol and Noah equally desperate to help her. Even after they'd connected in person and begun to date, they'd often wound up an evening with a phone conversation.

As Alex had grown stronger and more self-confident, she had dared to want more from Noah than a helping hand. And his passionate kisses had let her know that he had felt the same way. They'd been falling in love. She'd even been on the verge of inviting Noah to spend spring break at home with her when Elizabeth had summoned the gang to her room and announced that she was treating them all to this cruise on the *Homecoming Queen*.

Now Noah leaned against the railing. With the wind whipping his thick hair, he could have been posing for a cigarette ad—except, of course, that he detested cigarettes.

"If face-to-face isn't working, let's try standing side by side," he said.

Hope rising inside her, Alex joined him at the railing. He put his arm around her, but he didn't pull her close or turn to look at her.

Really, he hadn't looked at her since the ship had left shore—not the kind of looking you do when you're in love. Why?

Her hand stole up to her face. No bumps met

her fingertips; thanks to her twice-daily scrub ritual, she was zit-free. Still, out here in the Caribbean glare, the absence of makeup was downright scary.

She could see a shadow of stubble on Noah's cheeks, even though he shaved very closely. She happened to think it was a turn-on, but how did he feel about the freckles visible on her face? If someone had come along selling paper bags, she would have bought one and plopped it over her head.

At her side, Noah sighed expansively. "The sea is magnificent, isn't it?" He pointed toward the horizon. "It's the way the green fades to gray out there. If infinity has a color, there it is."

"Gee, Noah, if you ever want to moonlight, you could probably make a fortune naming cosmetics," Alex quipped. "I'd buy Infinity Green-Gray in a shot. Not that I don't think you'll succeed brilliantly as a psychologist," she added hastily, in case he thought she'd been expressing doubts.

Apparently he didn't think she'd been expressing anything, because he went on as though she hadn't said a word.

"I feel like one of the explorers heading for the new world," Noah said in a reflective voice. "I know the current theory is that they were motivated by greed, but even the worst of them must also have had tremendous courage. Heading into the cosmic nothingness."

I don't want to talk about the explorers, Alex thought. *I want to explore our cosmic somethingness.* Didn't he realize that?

When their relationship had been more like that of doctor and patient, Noah had seemed to know what she needed before she did. Where was his famous empathy now that she needed what any girl in love required—affection, admiration, and romance?

"I had my doubts about this trip," Noah continued relentlessly. "But I'm awfully glad I came. There's nothing like an ocean to put things in perspective."

Absolutely, Alex said to herself. An ocean did it every time. *That's why you're grooving on Christopher Columbus and I'm sweating bullets about my complexion.*

"We have a lot to learn from the waves," Noah proclaimed, sounding more and more like their psychology professor when he got carried away with a topic. "As a group, their behavior is so predictable—and yet each individual wave has its own characteristics."

"Maybe that can be your Ph.D. thesis," Alex said brightly. "The Ego, the Id, and the Waves."

Noah was too wound up to pay attention to her. "I think I'll have prints of Turner's seascapes in my office," he said decisively, as if it were an urgent matter that had to be resolved that second. "Nobody painted the ocean like Turner."

At that point Alex gave up. First the ocean, then the explorers, and now apparently she was in for an art-history lecture. But who could blame him?

She looked down at herself. The plain white T-shirt, loose white drawstring pants, and sockless white sneakers were a total flop. Rather than looking sophisticated and nautical, she looked like someone on a meditation retreat.

No, it was worse than that, she realized, her heart constricting. She looked like Enid. *No wonder he doesn't want anything to do with me.*

Alex had been Enid until she'd gotten to SVU last fall. The change in name had confused her old friends for a while, but it was the smartest thing she'd ever done. A new wrapping for a new package. A new title for a new book. Because SVU hadn't been just another step on the path. It had been a major turning point. A leap.

Of course, she'd had some major problem as Alex, too. But she'd gotten through the obstacles, and she didn't want to go back to being Enid. That was one of many things that Noah had helped her to understand about herself—back when they were communicating.

Since there were no telephones here to help

her get in touch with him, she'd just have to show him. He obviously needed a dose of the glamorous Alex to remind him that he was supposed to be kissing her, not giving her academic lectures.

"Meet me in the Venetian Lounge in an hour," she said authoritatively. Before he could get so much as another glimpse of Enid, she turned and fled toward the stairwell.

Chapter Four

"Quando sei qui con me, questa stanza non a piu paretti, ma àlberi—"

Lila's eyes flew open. The singing wasn't in her mind. As a striking man in a well-cut linen suit approached her, a sad smile on his face, her heart pounded and her breath caught in her throat. But this time the sight of Leonardo didn't make Lila faint; it made her squirm.

She wished she weren't wearing only a shocking pink bikini and flimsy cotton blanket. She'd counted on not seeing Leonardo until noon, when she would appear in the full countess regalia—a wide-brimmed straw hat, long pearls, panty hose, and strappy sandals. And a dress, of course. Ivory linen, with long sleeves.

She sneaked a look at her wristwatch. Twenty after twelve! Doing nothing certainly took a lot of time.

"*Buon giorno*, Lila," Leonardo greeted her. He gave a courtly bow in her direction. "I hope you don't mind that I tracked you down here. My pilot is supposed to pick me up at three, and we have much to discuss."

Lila wriggled into the most dignified posture she could manage. "*Buon giorno*, Leonardo. I'm so sorry I'm late for our meeting. It's the sun—it always puts me to sleep."

"You are feeling better today?"

"Much better, thank you. It was quite a shock seeing you last night, I have to admit."

"Clearly," he said with a small smile. "I am so sorry that my wire never reached the ship to warn you of my arrival."

"Your cabin was comfortable?"

He sat down gingerly on an adjoining chaise, adjusting the back into its upright position. "Quite adequate. For a student ship the accommodations are better than one might expect."

Lila had to swallow a giggle. Leonardo was so stuffy! Although his English was terrific—better than Tisiano's had been—it lacked the charm of his brother's speech.

Maybe it was just the context, she told herself, urging herself to be charitable. Probably if she'd met him in Italy, she'd have thought he was great.

Her thoughts were dispersed by the unmistakable—and totally unexpected—sound of metal clashing on wood. Rollerblades. Lila grinned as four kids from some other college came speeding down the deck in a rainbow of neon spandex. When they saw her, they skidded to a halt.

"It's our physics project," one of them called. "Seeing what the ship's momentum does to the old newtons." He held up a piece of cardboard with a spinner and some numbers on it. "Want to measure the force of our momentum?"

Lila had no idea what he was talking about, but whatever the group was doing, it looked like fun. She would have been tempted to join in, except that Leonardo was staring at her and the skaters as if they were extraterrestrials.

"Sorry, I can't," she said regretfully. "But I hope you get an A."

As the other kids took off with a friendly wave, Leonardo's frown deepened. *"Signora,"* he began, with a severe formality. "I do not comprehend it. If I had not been here, you would have gone with them, *sì*?"

Lila sat up straighter. "I might have," she said in a soft voice.

"But you are La Contessa di Mondicci," he protested. "You are my brother's widow. Have you no pride? Have you no grief?"

Lila remembered that before she had been a countess, she'd been Ms. Lila Fowler. And Lila

43

Fowler didn't take lessons in comportment from anybody.

"Don't give me any grief about grief," she retorted before she could censor herself. His look of bewilderment deepened, and she paused. "Mourning is very personal, Leonardo," she finally said in a gentler voice. "You chose not to come to the funeral. Did I give you a hard time about that?"

"You know that I was in China on business. I didn't come because you arranged for it to happen so quickly," he protested.

"There was time for you to get there if you really wanted to," Lila said. "I think maybe you didn't want to see me. You preferred to wait and have your own memorial when the American interloper was gone."

Leonardo didn't say anything, and she gestured toward the big manila envelope he had in his hand. "Let's get down to business," she suggested, in a tone she had learned from hearing her father deal with his lawyers and accountants.

Bruce chose that moment to reappear with the drink that Lila had requested. He'd changed into purple swim trunks and a short white jacket he had obviously bribed one of the stewards into lending him. He carried the drink on a regulation waiter's tray, and Lila couldn't help laughing.

"Sorry it took me so long," Bruce said as he approached.

Lila saw Bruce's gaze fall on Leonardo, who was gaping at Bruce as if he were an apparition.

"Oh, hi, Len," Bruce said breezily. "If I'd known you were coming, I'd have brought you a drink. What's your pleasure? A glass of Verdicchio? Or is it more a day for Montepulcianno?"

"Thank you, Mr.—Batman, is it?" His tone was scathing.

Lila and Bruce laughed at the mistake, but Leonardo's lips didn't so much as quiver. If he'd meant to be funny, he wasn't about to let on.

"Patman, Len," Bruce said, seeming to take great delight in the other man's obvious abhorrence of the American-style nickname. "That's *P* as in pepperoni pizza, *A* as in artichoke, *T*—"

Lila sent him an urgent signal. Bruce was going too far. She didn't want to offend Leonardo's delicate sensibility *too* much. "Bruce, it really would be nice if you got a drink for my brother-in-law. Something refreshing, like this." She took an appreciative sip from the glass of fruity mineral water he'd brought her. "We need a few minutes to talk business."

"Sure thing," Bruce replied easily. "Whatever you say." He made a small bow. "At your service, *bella contessa*."

He was scarcely out of earshot before Leonardo grimaced. "What a ridiculous young man."

Lila glowered. "That ridiculous young man

45

saved my life when we were in a plane crash together."

"A plane crash that was probably his own fault," Leonardo returned.

Lila was sure that the bright blush spreading across her face told Leonardo that there was some truth to his last statement.

"Has he been saving your life since the plane crash?" Leonardo asked, his eyes burning into hers.

"That's none of your business!"

The darkly handsome Italian waved the manila envelope. "I'm afraid it is. Thanks to the arrangement of Tisiano's estate, your business and my business are one and the same."

"Oh, I see." Lila nodded knowingly. "This is one of those soap operas in which the widowed countess has to pawn her diamonds because her husband's family doesn't approve of her. *Mi dispiace,* Leonardo. I'm sorry. You're going to need a new scriptwriter."

He looked taken aback, but she didn't stop. "As you can easily find out by getting a financial profile of my family, I'm loaded in my own right," she stated crisply. "I didn't marry Tisiano for his money, and I don't need it now. But if he wanted me to have it, I think I should have it. So maybe I better arrange for one of my father's lawyers to fly down and meet us."

To her surprise, Leonardo groaned. "*Dio mio,* how did we get off on such a footing? Lila, I am so sorry. I did not mean to suggest that I thought you a fortune hunter. It's just—" He choked and seemed unable to continue for a moment. "It's just that I miss him so much," he finally got out. Leonardo's arrogant features softened, and he began to sob.

As if a key had been turned, opening the floodgates, Lila felt tears begin to course down her cheeks. "I miss him too."

"All my life, he was the person on earth I loved the most," Leonardo said brokenly. "But in one way we were very different. I have always been so quick to get restless with a woman. I suppose that's why I run a modeling agency—so I have an excuse to dart from Milan to Peking to San Juan, looking for someone more beautiful and exciting than the woman before."

Lila nodded, listening. Leonardo appeared to be a more complex man than she'd guessed.

An affectionate smile brightened his face. "Tisiano was different. He was always looking for his great love. In you, I believe, he found it. That's why I am shocked to see you so—indifferent."

"I'm not indifferent!" Lila exclaimed. "I cried so much those first few weeks, I'm amazed my body didn't turn to dust. But—"

"But what?"

47

"But I'm only eighteen! I loved him, but I didn't die with him." Her eyes beseeched her brother-in-law for understanding. "I have a right to a life."

"Yes," he returned fervently. "I know Tisiano would want that. But so soon, Lila? As you say, you are very young. You have so much time stretching out in front of you. Couldn't you have spared a year to remember your husband? Did you have to jump out of your mourning clothes and into a bikini quite so quickly? And into the arms of that absurd young man?"

This time Lila didn't rise to Bruce's defense. A slow flush of shame stealing across her cheeks, she thought of how briefly, indeed, she had mourned.

She'd welcomed her parents' and friends' advice to put the past behind her. And she'd been more than willing to toss away the black dresses and hats that invited somber looks and hushed conversation.

She looked at Leonardo, stricken with grief. Staring deeply into his melancholy eyes, she shuddered at the Lila she saw reflected—a shallow American child.

She'd been a good wife, but she was a disaster as a widow. The man who'd died with her name on his lips deserved more from her.

"Leonardo, you've given me a lot to think about," she said with quiet dignity. "I thought it was enough to honor Tisiano's memory in my heart, but maybe I was wrong."

The sadness in Lila's voice seemed to touch Leonardo. "And perhaps I was too harsh," he said.

"No, I deserved your words," she responded. "I really did."

Rising, he kissed her hand. "I can see now why my brother married you. You have a gracious soul, Lila. We shall start all over again with each other, yes? After all, we have something important in common. We both loved the sweetest man who ever lived."

They made another appointment, for two o'clock in the Venetian Lounge, and Leonardo left Lila to her thoughts. They weren't happy thoughts, but they felt like the right ones. In fact, they were the only thoughts possible under the circumstances.

Lila pulled on the jacket that matched her bikini. She buttoned all the buttons. If she encountered Bruce before she had a chance to change, she wanted her appearance to help back up her words.

She knew exactly what she was going to say to him. She silently rehearsed her delivery, steeling herself not to weaken no matter how much he protested.

And she was sure he would protest—because she had a pretty rough message for him. "I love you, Bruce, and I hate to hurt you, but I owe something to Tisiano. I have to grieve a little longer. I love you, Bruce, and it's over."

"Which way is ze airport?" The souvenir vendor flashed a dazzling grin and pointed as he echoed Bryan Nelson's question.

Bryan's gaze followed the other man's finger. It was extended in the same direction the SS *Homecoming Queen* was headed—out to sea.

Bryan silently cursed the language barrier. He asked the question again, twice as slowly and four times as loudly, as if he were addressing a particularly resistant child. "I don't think you understood. Which way is the airport?" He practically shouted the last few words.

Just to make his meaning totally clear, he flapped his arms up and down.

"I am zorry, zir," the other man said. He flapped his own arms, and now he made no effort to choke back his laughter. "We do not have an airport. So you will have to go to Juma. Zat-a-way." And once again he pointed toward the ocean.

Bryan was wildly tempted to take the man's brightly colored postcards and toss them into the air. Instead, he took a deep breath and forced himself to remain calm.

He did his best to produce an ingratiating smile. "And how do I get to Juma?"

The vendor laughed. He eyed Bryan's tall, muscular physique. "You are a good swimmer, yes?"

Bryan's hands inched toward the postcards. Just what he needed! The vendor was obviously relishing Bryan's misery.

But this wasn't about human relations. It was about his relationship with the ocean. An extremely uneasy relationship, at that.

"I don't swim," Bryan said through clenched teeth. "Nor do I walk on water."

"Zen it is a very good zing zat we have boats. Down by ze dock you will find plenty of people who will take you." The vendor looked at Bryan's bag. "Zome of zem will even have room for your zootcase. Maybe."

Bryan looked at the boats in question and realized that his tormentor wasn't kidding. Bryan had been in bathtubs bigger than most of those so-called boats.

Bryan's whole life passed before his eyes, just the way it would again when the waters closed over his head. Here came his parents and sisters. And wow, his first-grade teacher. *Hi, Mrs. DuBois. Guess what? I did learn to read.*

Why hadn't he learned to swim instead? Not that any sane person would have struck out into the shark-laden waters, but at least he could have faced a boat. As it was, there was no way he could

51

head into the open sea in something about as sturdy as a plywood model ship. He stared longingly at the wake churning behind the *Homecoming Queen*.

"Nina!" he wanted to cry out. "Don't leave me here! I'll never be a jerk again, I promise!"

He really had been a jerk, all right. Everything he'd done since they'd lifted anchor had been supremely jerky—especially getting hit in the head with a shuffleboard puck. It wasn't the wound that was so bad; it was the cure. He'd gotten four stitches from the capable hands of Richard Daniels, M.D., who'd apparently sewed up Nina Harper's interest along with Bryan's scalp.

Which had led to Nina and Richard's parasailing adventure. And seeing Nina having a great time with the doctor had fueled Bryan's decision to leave the ship and fly back to Sweet Valley—the jerkismo decision of all.

As the ship receded, so did his spirits. Somehow it made him feel even worse that the souvenir vendor had stopped chuckling and was looking at him with something that suspiciously resembled pity.

"You want a ginger beer?" the man offered. He took a bottle out of a glass-front refrigerator. "Much better than American cola. Make everyzing feel better."

"Does it have alcohol in it?" The last thing

Bryan needed was to get drunk. He already felt as if the world were spinning too quickly.

"No alcohol," the vendor assured him. "It's like ginger ale, but better. Much zingier."

Bryan nodded and took out his wallet. "And some postcards, please. A dozen of them," he said hurriedly as a flock of tourists, no doubt thirsty, came up behind him. "I don't care which ones."

Dear Nina, If we never meet again, I just want you to know . . .

Dear fellow members of the Black Students Union, I hope you'll carry on the good fight . . .

The ginger beer was so good that he drank it too fast and it went up his nose. As he sneezed and sputtered, he had to laugh.

I don't need the Caribbean to drown in. I'm going to be the first guy to suffocate himself with a soft drink!

The Venetian Lounge was certainly a place where a girl wanted to look her best, Alex thought. There was so much reflecting glass in the room, it was like being in a fun house—except that all the mirrors in the lounge were definitely user friendly.

The pillar near their table, for instance, was covered with thin vertical strips of mirror, so that when Alex shook her head even slightly, her hair seem to fan out and float like a beautiful reddish

53

gold cloud. Stealing an admiring glance at the pillar, she was glad she'd made the extra effort to turn her head upside down and brush her hair from underneath, giving it body.

And the ornately framed mirror opposite their table sent back another message that all effort she'd made had paid off. Putting on a little foundation had turned her skin to alabaster. And leaving the blush off her wide cheekbones—a trick she'd just read about in a magazine—forced the viewer to focus on her eyes. She hoped that Noah was noticing her Infinity Gray-Green eyelids. She blinked them a couple of times to attract his attention.

Nothing happened.

A lot of other guys in the lounge were casting admiring glances her way. But the guy who claimed to love her was scowling at her.

Catching a reflected glimpse of the well-stocked bar behind her, Alex realized that it was a very good thing she no longer depended on alcohol to get her through tense moments. And of course, her sober status was due in great part to Noah's tender loving care.

She really wanted to let him know how much he meant to her. She couldn't offer him the kind of insights he'd generously given her, but she could help him relax and enjoy life a little—if he'd let her.

If she had her way, he'd feel good about himself just because he was sharing a fresh orangeade with a bouncy-haired girl who was crazy about him.

Well, subtle, smoldering glances were getting her nowhere. If she didn't get a little more aggressive, Noah was going to spend the rest of his life crumpling and recrumpling the two inches of wrapper that had capped the straw in his glass.

"I've never been in the real Venice," she said. "Have you?"

He shook his head.

Angling her own head, Alex drew his attention to the big, bright mural of gondoliers on the Grand Canal.

"It certainly would be fun to be in a gondola together, wouldn't it?" she said brightly.

Noah nodded.

This is going nowhere fast, Alex said to herself. She racked her brain for inspiration. Maybe he needed some flattery. After all, even future psychologists probably suffered from low self-esteem once in a while.

"I don't know if you noticed my eyelids," she said, "but you inspired them. When you talked about the ocean being the color of infinity."

He stared at her. "I was talking about things that really mattered to me, and all you could think about was eye shadow?"

"Of course not, Noah. I really like how cosmic your mind is. But sometimes it's nice to capture a little piece of the cosmos." She sat back, waiting for him to agree with her. But instead of a smile, she got a frown.

"I hope you're aware that narcissism is a very serious personality disorder," he said soberly.

"Narcissism!"

"Named for the guy who was so in love with his own face that he leaned too far over a brook to see his reflection—"

"I know who Narcissus was, Noah! And don't you dare go around diagnosing me! You'll lose your psychologist's license before you even get it." She took a long, angry swallow of orangeade. "You don't like what I'm saying because you think you're the only one who's qualified to come up with any theories. Talk about narcissism!"

Folding his hands behind his head, he tipped back his chair. "All right, let's talk about it."

She stared at him in disbelief. Had he eaten something for breakfast that had the power to turn a great guy into an idiot? They were in the most romantic setting imaginable, and he was turning their time together into a therapy session!

Was that how he saw her—as the perpetual patient? A wounded child who needed his help and had nothing to give in return?

A waiter crossed her field of vision, a pair of

frozen strawberry margaritas on his tray. It was the thick frosting of salt on the rim of the glasses that got to her. She could imagine the sting of the salt against her lips, followed by the numbing sweetness of ice-cold liquid. Maybe she deserved a little anesthesia.

No, Alex! Don't give in! Get out of here!

Tears blurring her eyes, Alex pushed back her chair and fled toward the exit. And ran smack into the cool, linen-jacketed chest of a man coming through the doorway.

Chapter Five

"Winston, is it a mirage? Or is that the one and only Bryan Nelson?"

Winston Egbert flashed one of those affectionate grins that made Denise Waters feel ten feet tall. "I love you madly," he said, "but I'm not ready for mirage."

Denise scrunched up her face. "Winnie, that's possibly the worst pun I've ever heard."

"You don't like my sense of humor? I thought laughter was one of the best things in our relationship."

"Oh, never mind," she said, ruffling his hair. "This is no time to discuss our relationship. Move!"

Denise grabbed his hand and broke into a run before he could protest. Winston and Bryan's stars were definitely crossed. Whenever the two guys were in close proximity, accident-prone Winston was sure to set a disaster in motion, and Bryan had a habit of being in its way.

"Yo, Bryan! Hi! Over here!" As they caught up to him, Denise slowed. "You missed the boat too? We were having so much fun making calypso music, we lost track of the time. What were you doing, buying a present for Nina?"

"Not exactly. I, uh, jumped ship. I decided to fly back to SVU."

"Oh, Bryan." Denise hugged him. "What's up? I thought you'd already survived everything bad that could happen to you on this trip. Which reminds me, how's your head?"

"My head's okay." Bryan smiled reassuringly. "It's my heart that hurts."

"Aw, come on, Bryan," Winston said. "You're not worried about that guy in the white coat, are you?"

"Me, worry about a yuppie healer who makes two hundred thousand dollars a year and parasails? That wouldn't worry you, Winston, would it?"

"Not for a second," Winston assured him as he grabbed Denise and wrapped his arms around her. "That's it. Forget about the ship. We—" He skidded to a halt. "Bryan, did I hear you say 'fly'? There's an airport here? As in, helicopter back to the *Homecoming Queen*?"

Bryan looked sheepish. "Ze airport is not on zees island."

"What was that?" Denise asked, a confused expression on her face.

Bryan pointed out to sea. "It's over there. On Juma."

"Which is also where the *Queen* stops next," Winston said. "So we travel together. Fun!"

"That's the trouble," Bryan said. "Travel how? Seems there's no way of getting to Juma—except by toy boat."

"Funny you should mention it," Winston said. "Do you know it's impossible to say 'toy boat' five times fast without getting tongue-tied? Go ahead, try it."

Denise gave Winston a sharp look. She loved her boyfriend, but sometimes he didn't know when to stop being a clown. She turned her head and looked into Bryan's eyes. "It's no go with the little boats?"

"No go. To tell you the truth, the mere thought of being in one of those things is petrifying."

"I've seen you read sci-fi—can't you just warp yourself there or something?" Bryan looked so miserable that Denise hugged him again. "I didn't mean to tease you. I guess I was really trying to say that you have such a terrific mind, can't you think your way around your fear?"

61

"It's not my mind that's the problem," Bryan said. "It's my feet. They keep just saying no."

"We could knock you unconscious," Winston offered helpfully. "And bring you around after we land on Juma."

Bryan grabbed his wounded head. "With my luck, I'd end up in the hands of Dr. Daniels again." The name came out as a snarl. "That guy and me and a scalpel in the same room—not a good idea. No way."

Denise decided it was time to take charge. "Then we just have to find a big boat," she said decisively. "A seaworthy vessel. We have to, so we will. Come on, guys. Before the ship gets to Juma and takes off again without us."

"Alex! Are you okay?"

"Oh, hi, Lila. I'm—I'm so sorry," Alex stammered, directing her words to the tall, well-built man with whom she'd just collided.

Lila noted that Alex was staring at Leonardo as if he were a movie star. It was the same reaction many women had had to Tisiano.

"No, it is I who must apologize, *signorina*," he said. "I must have been blinded by your beauty. Are you quite all right?"

"I'm wonderful," Alex said slowly as she gazed into the deep pools of his eyes.

"Alex, may I present Leonardo di Mondicci,

62

Tisiano's younger brother?" Lila said formally. "Leonardo, I'd like you to meet an old friend, Alexandra Rollins."

"Oh, not so old," Leonardo said as Lila looked at him in amazement.

So the guy has some wit, after all, Lila thought. *How interesting.*

Leonardo kissed Alex's hand. *"Piacere, signorina,"* he murmured.

"And this is Noah Pearson," Lila went on as Noah got up from his table and joined them, an unreadable expression on his face. "Noah, meet Leonardo di Mondicci."

Lila had no trouble reading the expression on the face of her brother-in-law, however. He looked as though he'd just discovered America. Even while he was shaking hands perfunctorily with Noah, his stare was fixed on Alex's cheekbones.

"You'll have to excuse us, guys," Lila said to Alex and Noah. "Leonardo and I have some complicated business to discuss, and he's getting picked up at three o'clock."

"No, no, no." Leonardo clucked. "We have all the time in the world. I've decided that you have the right idea, *cara* Lila. A cruise is so restorative after a tragic loss. I plan to radio my pilot not to come this afternoon. I shall remain for the rest of the voyage. After all, I have someone very precious to keep my eye on."

He linked a fraternal arm through Lila's, patting her hand. But he didn't fool her for a second. He'd be keeping one eye on his sister-in-law all right. But his other eye would stay glued to Alex.

"What do you want to do?" Danny asked Isabella.

"I don't know. What do you want to do?"

Danny grinned. "I don't know. What do you want to do?"

They both laughed, and Danny thought gratefully of all the different ways that Isabella had taught him to have fun—like quoting favorite lines from old movies.

He stole a look at Jason to see if he'd caught on that Danny and Isabella had just played a scene from that great fifties film *Marty,* in which characters kept asking each other what they wanted to do. Jason could talk for hours about his love for Nicole, but he didn't always act like a man in love.

Not that a guy had to dance before his beloved with a rose between his teeth. But Danny felt strongly that every couple should engage in the kind of affectionate playfulness that went on between him and Isabella when things were going well.

And they were going well right now. For a few hours, relations had been strained. Then he'd calmed down Isabella with his promise to say nothing to Jason about the kiss between Tom and Nicole. And she'd calmed him down by agreeing that the bride and groom seemed to need a lesson in capital-*R* Romance.

Danny had proposed to Jason that the two couples have an afternoon double date. Now they were sitting at a table in the Café de Paris, the ship's espresso bar, trying to figure out where to go next.

"So what do you want to do, Jason?" Danny asked.

"Gee, I don't know. Maybe you and I should go work out in the gym. I've been eating enough for five guys. There isn't much to do around here except gorge on fattening food."

Nicole rolled her eyes. "Do you believe this guy? Nothing to do?" She reached for Jason's hand. "How about sitting next to each other in the nice, dark movie theater, sharing a bag of pop-corn?"

"More food," Jason muttered.

"What's showing?" Danny asked. "Some-thing"—he cleared his throat—"romantic?"

Isabella put down her glass mug of cappuccino. "I saw a pile of program calendars on that table near the door. I'll be right back."

She returned a moment later. "It's *A Night to Remember*—about the sinking of the *Titanic*," she announced.

"Whoever arranged the schedule has a sense of humor," Danny commented.

"A disaster flick," Jason said. "I know that's not Nicole's kind of thing, but maybe you and I can go, Danny."

"I don't know about sitting in the dark when there's all that great sunshine up on deck," Danny said quickly. "I'd rather check out the miniature golf. There's something romantic about a floating golf course, isn't there? Do you play, Nicole?"

"I never have," she said, "but I bet I could learn."

"Especially if you have a pro like Jason here to put his arms around you and help you with your swing," Danny said enthusiastically.

"Nah," said Jason. "I've gotten to be a pretty serious golfer, you know. My handicap's down to four. Minigolf is just for amateurs."

Your handicap is that you're a bonehead, Danny wanted to say. *You keep telling us you're wildly in love, but you don't show it.*

"If you think you need a workout, maybe we should all go to the pool," he remarked instead. "There's nothing more romantic than having a certain someone put the sunblock on your back, is there?"

"Actually, I'm just getting over an ear infection," Jason said. "So I probably shouldn't go swimming."

Danny felt as if he were digging himself deeper and deeper into a hole. But he decided to give romance one more try. He gestured at the Toulouse-Lautrec posters that decorated the wood-paneled café.

"Look at those scenes of Paris. Hey, it's still got to be the most romantic city in the world, don't you think, Jason?"

"If you think it's romantic to be ripped off," Jason answered. "This friend of mine went last summer, and he paid ten dollars for a lemonade. Do you believe it?"

"No, I don't believe it," Danny mumbled, determined not to say another word about anything. He signaled the waiter and ordered another espresso and a croissant. Maybe if he kept his mouth stuffed with food, he'd stop putting his foot into it.

Tom Watts sat on his bunk bed, his head in his hands. He hadn't felt this miserable in a long, long time. Just when he'd thought his luck had finally turned around for good, he'd lost the two people who mattered most in the world—his girlfriend and his best friend.

It was unbelievable, but it was undeniable. Elizabeth had told him to get lost as if he were a wild dog foaming at the mouth. And Danny was giving him the silent treatment.

The two people he cared about the most weren't just angry at him. This wasn't one of those little misunderstandings that was going to end in a communal burst of laughter.

Elizabeth Wakefield and Danny Wyatt hated him. Tom was used to having enemies. He could even take pleasure in being hated—by people he hated back. But it wasn't that psychopath William White staring daggers at him now. It was Elizabeth. And Danny. It hurt like hell.

Tom leafed listlessly through the book of eighteenth-century verse he'd put into his suitcase—just in case he needed something stirring to whisper into Elizabeth's ear. The words that leaped up at him were stirring, all right:

> As the earth when leaves are dead,
> As the night when sleep is sped,
> As the heart when joy is fled,
> I am left alone, alone.

The world had turned upside down and inside out since Shelley had penned those lines, but the human heart hadn't changed. It was still capable of throbbing with infinite pain.

Not since his entire family had been wiped out in a car crash had he felt so abandoned. And it wasn't fair. It wasn't as if he deserved such severe punishment.

Compassion was a good thing, wasn't it? It was one of the characteristics that Elizabeth and Danny theoretically admired in him. So what was compassionate Tom supposed to do when Nicole more or less fell apart right in front of him? Just hand her a broom and say, "Sweep yourself up"?

Anyone but the coldest-hearted creep would have put his arms around her.

So maybe there was a grain of passion in the compassion. He was allowed to be human, wasn't he? He'd never advertised himself as an angel. He had a past, like just about everyone else on this ship, and if the past had turned into the present for all of thirty seconds, was that supposed to signal the end of life as he knew it?

He hadn't planned for a girl he'd dated a few years ago to turn up on this cruise. And it wasn't his fault that she had her doubts about marrying a guy who seemed more interested in his friends than he was in her.

But nobody had given Tom a chance to explain.

If it had been Elizabeth and Todd up there on the deck, would he have exploded? He'd have been upset. Who wouldn't be? But he'd have given her a chance to talk before willing her into Siberia. And if she'd said it had just been a mistake and didn't mean a thing, he'd have forgiven her in a second. At least he wanted to think he would have.

Because he loved her. And believed in her love for him. Which was why knowing that he'd been a total and complete jerk was so hard to bear.

> *My heart each day desires the morrow,*
> *Sleep itself is turned to sorrow,*
> *Vainly would my winter borrow*
> *Sunny leaves from any bough.*

Tom closed the book of poetry with a bang. He wasn't going to spend the rest of the cruise in the company of Percy Bysshe Shelley. No matter what lengths he had to go to, Tom was going to prove to Elizabeth that he loved her.

Isabella stared ruefully at her cappuccino cup. Except for an unappealing residue of cinnamon-flecked steamed milk around the rim, it was conspicuously empty. She felt a wild urge to wave it under Danny's nose. *I'm here too*, she wanted to say. *Remember me?*

It was true that Danny had his hands full trying to instruct Jason in the ways of romance. But a good teacher had to do more than tell. He had to show.

Although she was anything but the frail type, it would be nice every once in a while not to have to fend for herself. As old-fashioned and prefeminist as her mind-set might be, it would be very nice to hear Danny say, "And another cappuccino for the lady, please."

Now that would be romantic.

Come to think of it, when was the last time Professor Romantic had practiced what he was preaching?

There were plenty of sparks flying between them. She definitely didn't have to look elsewhere for kisses. But maybe passion was one thing and romance quite another.

And maybe she'd once gotten both from Danny and now she was only getting one. Which put her way ahead of Nicole, apparently. But not where she wanted to be.

Are we losing it? she thought frantically. They were attracted to each other, they liked each other, they loved each other . . . but were they still in love? *Does Danny take me for granted?*

All at once it seemed the most important thing in the world to know. Even more urgent than getting another cappuccino, pronto.

Chapter Six

Jason slowed to a walk as he crossed the mile marker on the ship's oval jogging track. "Now that's what I call a run, man!"

He and Danny had just sweated and grunted their way to a respectable time of seven minutes and a few seconds. Danny had run with faster men, but he couldn't recall running with anyone more pleased with himself.

As soon as Danny and Jason had dropped off Isabella and Nicole at the miniature golf course, Jason's mood had rapidly begun to improve. By the time they'd done their first few laps around the track, Jason had been whistling to himself. Did Jason realize how much happier he seemed without Nicole around?

"I wish Nicole had seen that last sprint!" Jason said, compounding Danny's confusion. "Pretty good form, huh?"

"Yeah, and not bad in the modesty department, either," Danny said, slapping his friend on the shoulder. Whatever Jason's problem was, it wasn't low self-esteem.

Jason propped himself against a wall and pulled his right leg up behind him to stretch it. "It's hard to be modest when you have a great babe who's nuts about you. You know what that's all about."

"At the risk of sounding politically correct, Isabella's an extremely intelligent woman and wouldn't appreciate me referring to her as a 'babe,'" Danny said. "Not that I mind her being the prettiest woman in the world, but there's a lot more to her than that."

"Second prettiest," Jason said. "I've got the first. Nicole really is beautiful, isn't she?"

Danny nodded. "She must turn a lot of heads," he couldn't help saying. The comment wasn't technically a break of his promise to Isabella, but he was glad she wasn't there to hear him.

"She sure does. Guys hit on her all the time. I wouldn't admit it to anyone but my best man, but I sort of get a kick out of it. Especially because I know she'd never cheat on me."

A groan escaped Danny's lips. "Ouch, my calf," he improvised quickly. He bent down and vigorously massaged his lower right leg.

Danny was silent as he and Jason headed toward the locker room. He'd been in tough spots before, but never like this. On the one hand, he'd promised Isabella to butt out of Jason and Nicole's relationship. On the other hand, he had a responsibility to keep Jason from getting hurt.

It didn't make the situation any simpler that Jason seemed more in love with the idea of Nicole than with Nicole herself. He was seeming more and more like a guy who was acquiring a trophy wife rather than marrying a real, live woman. Maybe he deserved what he was getting.

And maybe he didn't.

Of course he didn't!

Maybe he did.

Isabella, help! What am I supposed to do?

Isabella didn't answer, but as he stepped into the shower, Danny suddenly had an inspiration.

He would save Jason from faithless Nicole and Nicole from self-centered Jason, and he would do it without risking his relationship with Isabella.

Because he would do it ethically.

Somehow, some way, he would get Jason to break the engagement. But not by telling him about the kiss.

"You genius, Wyatt!" he called out into the cascading water.

Richard Daniels, M.D., was gazing so deeply into Nina Harper's eyes that she gave a self-conscious laugh and averted her own gaze.

"Hey," she protested lightly. "You're an internist, not an ophthalmologist. What's with the eye exam?"

His mouth quirked with pleasure. "All my life I've been looking for a woman who could correctly pronounce 'ophthalmologist.' Do you know how many people say that first syllable as if it were 'op' and not 'oph'?"

"How many?" she asked solemnly.

"Every single one of them except for you. I feel like the prince's courtier finally finding the one woman in all the land who could fit into the glass slipper."

"Oh, be honest, Richard. You feel like the prince, not his courtier."

Richard threw back his handsome head and laughed. "Touché. You got me. Can you forgive me?"

"For what, being arrogant?"

"No," he said, a shade more seriously. "For being everything your parents wanted you to find in a man."

He was so amazingly on target that it was Nina's turn to burst out laughing. "What did you do, hire a detective?"

"Didn't have to," he said smugly. "You don't have to be Dr. Freud to figure that one out. Am I right?"

Nina flushed. Her mother had been slow to take to Bryan and his radical politics, but she'd come to respect and like him. Like him very much. Still, Nina knew, Mrs. Harper would probably be slightly ecstatic at the thought of Nina with this upper-middle-class black success story sitting across from her—not only a doctor, but a great-looking, amusing one who sailed, skied, and had climbed the Matterhorn.

Nina had to admit that it had been a long time since she'd had a date she could write home about. A description of an afternoon with Bryan would depress any mother. *Dear Mom, Today Bryan read me a manifesto about everything wrong with the world. It was a brilliant manifesto, although I have to admit it sounded a lot like the one he read me last week. I wore those great red leggings you sent me, but he didn't seem to notice. In fact, I think he may have fallen in love with this new copying machine on campus. Any advice?*

A description of the past few hours would be a very different matter. Parasailing at their port of call, guiltlessly relaxing over tall glasses of mineral water . . . and Richard showering her with attention. He'd complimented her on everything from the blue and white beads woven into her braids to the coordinated blue and white socks on her feet.

"One of my professors in medical school was a wise man," Richard went on. "He said that being as how I would be considered God's gift to mother-in-laws, I'd better be sure that any daughters involved had gotten past the rebellious stage." He cupped Nina's right hand in both of his. "Well?"

Now it was her turn to perform an eye exam. And what she saw in the doctor's eyes was unnerving. Beneath the twinkle, she saw steadiness, purpose, and ambition—all focused on her!

He's not just handing me a line, she thought. *He really digs me.*

Her mind churned. Had Bryan been her rebellion—a rebellion she'd now passed through? And was he to be relegated to the past tense in her heart? Or was she still in love with him?

He'd been a stick-in-the-mud ever since the *Homecoming Queen* had left port, but that wasn't the end of the world, was it?

Or maybe it was. Maybe his inability to have fun—and his unwillingness to let her have fun— was anything but trivial.

Because how was she going to accomplish everything big she meant to do in her life if she didn't get to refresh her spirit now and then? How would she have enough spirit to face the challenges out there if she didn't get to relax at home?

Richard Daniels knew how to relax. Bryan Nelson didn't.

But maybe it was her role to teach him. . . .

She pictured Bryan back in Sweet Valley, ripe for consolation after a bummer of a vacation. He would have no trouble finding it, that was for sure.

Richard's voice gently penetrated her thoughts. "I seem to have asked the sixty-four-thousand-dollar question," he said. "So have you gotten past the rebellious stage or not?"

"I honestly don't know," Nina replied. "But I promise, if I figure out the answer before the cruise is over, I'll let you know."

"Hey, this doesn't have to be a shipboard romance," Richard said.

Nina picked up her glass and took a long swallow to cover her confusion. She wasn't even sure if she wanted to start something with this guy, and he was already telling her it didn't have to end.

"I'd like to try the climbing wall," she said, deciding to change the subject. "I hear it's moderately challenging and lots of fun."

"Not as challenging as you," Richard said. "And not half as much fun. But your wish is my command. Race you to the top, and the winner gets a kiss."

Bryan closed his eyes and cranked up his imagination. *I am Captain Nemo about to board the Nautilus,* he told himself, invoking the hero of a favorite science fiction novel, *Twenty Thousand Leagues Under the Sea.*

But when he opened his eyes, he was Bryan Nelson. And there was no way he was going to board the dinghy that was laughably named the

Jeanne d'Arc. Especially not in the company of accident-prone Winston Egbert!

Winston had already managed to send Bryan staggering off a pier and into the water—and the pier hadn't been moving.

"I'm sorry," he said tightly. "No can do."

Denise and Winston looked at each other and then back at him.

"We seem to have a genuine phobia on our hands," Denise said. Her voice was sympathetic, but she also sounded tired. And as discouraged as bubbly Denise was capable of sounding.

The threesome had trudged the entire length of the port. The *Jeanne d'Arc* was the most plausible rental boat they'd found—at least it had a motor. But the thought of getting in it made Bryan's mouth go as dry as cotton and his hands sweat.

He turned around and took stock of the harborside. Although souvenir stands and expensive boutiques predominated, some of the restaurants looked promising. And he spotted a small shop with a big sign advertising new and used books.

He knew what he had to do.

He swallowed hard. "You guys go ahead without me."

"We can't," Winston said.

"Really," Bryan insisted. "I'll be fine. The only way I'm going to get off this island is if you go first and send for me."

"I hate to admit it," Denise said, "but you're right. The minute we get to Juma, we'll head for the airstrip and hire a helicopter. You don't have a problem with small planes, do you?"

"Anything that flies is okay with me," Bryan said fervently.

"Human beings certainly are interesting," Winston said. "I get tense on an ordinary 747, but you'd probably feel cozy on a shuttle to the moon."

"I can't stand spiders," Denise confessed. "I was the only kid in my first-grade class who didn't love *Charlotte's Web*."

"Thanks for keeping me from feeling like a total wimp," Bryan said with a little laugh. "Now you better get going while there's still daylight. You're sure you'll be okay?"

"We'll be fine," Denise said. "The owner of the boat said the wind is favorable right now, and we should get there in an hour or two. Then we'll send for you."

"Bon voyage," Bryan said. "I'll be on the look-out."

He waved cheerily, but he couldn't help quaking inside. No one's survival should depend on Winston Egbert—least of all, his own.

"Hey, now there's a hot chick," Danny said as he steered Jason onto the sundeck that over-looked the pool. The sexist words almost stuck in his throat, but he managed to get them out.

"The redhead over there," Danny went on, pumping enthusiasm into his voice. "In the green bikini. Check her out."

Jason looked at him with surprise. "I thought you were a one-woman man."

"Oh, yeah, I am!" Danny agreed heartily. "But there's nothing wrong with looking, is there? It's like, um, in art history or something. I'm, ah, honing my aesthetic sensibility. Now that one over there, with the oval face—she looks like someone that what's-his-name would have painted. You know. Mondrian."

Jason burst out laughing. "Are you sure you take art history? Mondrian painted straight lines and right angles. Maybe you mean Modigliani?"

"That's it," Danny said. "Good old Modigliani. No straight lines on that one, huh?"

"Very nice," Jason said politely, sounding about as appreciative as a vegetarian who'd just been offered a lamb chop. "If you want to talk to her, don't mind me. I won't tell Isabella, if that's what you're worried about," he added when Danny hesitated.

Danny clapped a hand to his head. How had this gotten so turned around?

"I'd want you to tell Isabella," he said. "That would be the ethical thing to do, right? Unless, of course, you had an ethical reason not to." He noted that Jason was looking at him peculiarly. "But look, if you need for me not to say anything to Nicole—"

"There's nothing not to say to her," Jason said. He dismissed the entire poolside population with a sweep of his arm. "Nobody down there turns me on. I'm just not in the market anymore. I know lots of grooms have a last fling before they get married. But they don't have Nicole. And I do." His voice shimmered with pride.

That's what you think! Danny said inwardly.

"Which reminds me," Jason continued. "I want you to hold on to the wedding ring. That's part of the job description for the best man, right? It's a real beauty," he went on. "Set with diamond chips and seed pearls. It's been in my family since my great-grandmother wore it."

"Maybe you should keep it in the ship's vault," Danny said. "There are all these signs posted warning us not to leave valuables lying around."

"I trust you to keep it safe," Jason responded. "I'd trust you with my life, man."

Feeling about six inches tall, Danny followed Jason to his cabin and meekly put the ring in his pocket.

At least one thing's going right today, Bryan said to himself. The bookstore was a gold mine. There was reggae coming over the loudspeakers, a nice smell of old paper, and shelves crowded with unusual volumes.

He found two intriguing tracts about race relations in the Caribbean. Then he stumbled on a messy but incredibly varied section of bargain-priced used science fiction novels—Harlan Ellison, Robert Heinlein, and even an out-of-print Charles Platt. After a thorough search, Bryan spilled an armful of novels onto the checkout counter.

The bearded owner gave him the complicit grin of a fellow sci-fi reader. "You can have the whole bunch for ten dollars," he said, not bothering to add up the prices.

"Thanks!" Bryan replied, feeling upbeat for the first time since his blowout with Nina. He reached into the pocket where he kept his wallet.

A chilling emptiness greeted his hand.

Stay calm, he urged himself as he reached into other pockets.

But when he'd searched every pocket twice and scoured the bookshelves where he'd been hanging out, calmness deserted him.

"Someone must have pickpocketed me," he said with a groan. "What am I going to do?"

The friendly bookstore owner instantly turned indifferent. "Sorry, pal. I don't negotiate. I offered you a bargain."

Bryan's mind raced. "It must have been after I

bought the ginger beer and postcards. I thought I felt someone jostle me when I put my wallet away."

"Tough break," the owner responded. He came out from behind the counter and conspicuously reshelved the books Bryan had selected.

Bryan walked out of the bookstore, slamming the door behind him. What if Denise and Winston couldn't find a helicopter on Juma? He was marooned on this island. Without so much as the price of a ginger beer!

Chapter Seven

Danny held the heirloom wedding ring up to the light. "Wow!" he said, looking at the sparkle. "That's one sensational ring."

"For one sensational woman." Jason grinned.

"I hate to sound crass," Danny said. "But it looks as though it's worth a small fortune. It's insured, I hope."

"Of course, but its real value is sentimental. It goes back to the Pierces in Ireland."

As Danny returned the ring to its velvet-lined box, inspiration struck again. "I guess you won't be getting Nicole a lot of jewelry from now on," he commented.

"What do you mean?" Jason asked.

"Marriage is awfully expensive, isn't it? You've got to have, um, furniture and everything. Paintings for the walls. I mean, you can't just have posters when you're married. And—you know—you need vacuum cleaners and stuff like that. You have any idea how much a good vacuum cleaner costs?"

Jason laughed. "No, and neither do you. But that's why bridal registries were invented. We won't get everything on our wish list, but we've got lots of relatives and family friends—grown-up friends, I mean. When they see that we've really gone and tied the knot, someone's sure to give us a vacuum cleaner."

"But food," Danny pushed on desperately. "Those serious dinners. You don't survive on fries and nachos when you're married."

"Hey, I appreciate the reality check, but we'll be fine. When we're living together, we'll actually save on rent and food. Besides, Nicole's got a great summer job with a law firm. Now I'm the one who's going to sound crass—but financially I'm way ahead on this deal." Jason flashed the familiar smug smile.

Danny ground his teeth. This was positively the most frustrating situation he'd ever gotten into! He was trying to save Jason's life, and Jason was refusing to be saved. And just when he really needed Isabella with him, she was against him.

If only he hadn't seen Tom kissing Nicole. Then he'd be living in ignorant bliss, just like Jason was. Instead of acting like a fool trying to get

Jason to realize he was making a mistake, Danny would be spending every minute with Isabella.

Danny rubbed his temples. There had to be an answer. There just had to be.

To make sure she still existed, Isabella looked into her mirror. She frowned at her reflection. Not only did she exist, she looked rather stunning. Her lemon-yellow sundress contrasted arrestingly with her sleek dark hair and freshly burnished tan.

It was a good thing that mirrors existed, she decided. Because if she had to depend on Danny Wyatt to confirm her being, she'd be seriously out of luck.

Isabella had enthusiastically signed on for the cruise, convinced that romance would be in the air. As the confidante of the groom, Danny would be charged up with new passion.

Well, he was, but not for her.

The only people he was paying the slightest attention to were Jason and Nicole, Nicole and Jason.

I've had it! Isabella fumed. *He's supposed to be a best man, not a nanny!*

Why tell it to her mirror? Isabella stomped out of her stateroom, determined to track Danny down and confront him.

But locating Danny was easier said than done, she realized fifteen fruitless minutes later. The ship was a labyrinth. She felt as if she were hunting a wily electronic quarry in a three-dimensional video game.

To make her search even more frustrating, wherever she went—the Café de Paris, the Ping-Pong area, the pool—she was told that she'd missed Danny and Jason by ten or fifteen minutes.

Isabella took an unfamiliar turn away from the pool. Suddenly she found herself in a long, narrow passageway that stretched on forever but seemed to go nowhere. She felt as though she'd stepped out of the maze and into the fourth dimension. *Where am I?* she thought a little nervously.

Then she breathed a sigh of relief as she glimpsed a familiar back and cascading blond hair.

"Jessica!" she was about to call, when her friend whirled around with a finger to her lips.

She saw that Jessica had a quarry of her own— a tall guy in a blue-and-white-striped shirt and white pants.

The guy disappeared through a doorway, and Jessica gleefully summoned Isabella.

"That's him!" Jessica whispered excitedly. "And I've got him cornered in the men's room." She pointed to the sign on the door. "My mystery man!"

Elizabeth idly picked up the glossy brochure lying on her desk. The stateroom in the photograph might have been hers, with one important difference. The models in the picture were a man and a woman. And they were smiling at each other. Clearly the couple was eager to rumple one of the perfectly made beds. Tearing her eyes away from their faces, Elizabeth read aloud the caption: "Superb single and double accommodations to suit your budget and your personal desires. Each cabin has a private bath, spacious closet, porthole, and such amenities as a hair dryer, clothesline, and filtered drinking water."

Elizabeth let the brochure drop to the floor. "Personal desires," she repeated bitterly. Tom had certainly been up-front about his personal desires for this trip.

When he'd gone to pick up the tickets, he'd helped out the busy travel agent by sitting down at the computer and taking care of the accommodations. But instead of assigning Jessica and Elizabeth to a cabin, he'd given Jessica a single and put himself and Elizabeth together.

Elizabeth had been furious, and Tom hadn't made her feel better by telling her he'd thought that was what she wanted. She'd coldly explained that she would have discussed it with him if she'd wanted to take such a big step. She wouldn't have just gone ahead and set it up.

And that was true . . . up to a point. It was also true that she was madly attracted to him—or had been, before she'd seen him and Nicole kissing. And maybe if she'd had the guts to admit how much she wanted him, that kiss never would have happened.

As she looked around the cabin, Elizabeth couldn't help imagining how it would look if Tom's socks were on the floor instead of one of Jessica's bras. And if the razor on the sink in the bathroom were blue and straight rather than pink and curved. And if both pillows were on one bed.

It would look wonderful, she admitted to herself. *It would look like heaven.*

So why had she said no?

Not—as her sister thought—because she was a priss. A priss wouldn't melt when the guy she loved put his arms around her and pressed his lips to hers.

She hadn't said no just because of fear, either.

What had held her back was, well, the poetry factor. When she finally said yes to a man, the event would have to be perfect—a union as deep and starry as those that Lord Byron had set to verse. She wasn't going to do it just to do it. She didn't want any regrets to haunt her.

So she'd said no, and now she was haunted by regrets. And anger. And hurt. And guilt. And just about everything else unpleasant.

Sometimes being eighteen was unbearable. Ever since she'd gotten to college, Elizabeth had felt as if she were dancing on a tightrope. If she tumbled one way, she'd land back in childhood and be stuck there forever. If she fell the other way, she'd land in adulthood before she was ready.

She just had to keep on dancing, and Tom Watts had seemed the perfect partner.

She had thought he was different from all the other guys she'd dated. Maybe that was part of what made the situation so painful. She'd been in this position before—with Todd Wilkins. Maybe she and Todd would have parted anyway, but the breakup had definitely been sparked by her refusal to go to bed with him.

He'd quickly found consolation elsewhere. As Tom apparently had.

I'm just not ready, guys. And I'm not about to apologize for it!

Elizabeth picked up the brochure again and turned to the page that described "places to meet and eat." One caught her eye. "Feeling nostalgic for simpler times? Visit The Soda Fountain, an old-fashioned sweetshop with genuine fifties decor and jukebox. Don't forget your poodle skirt!"

Elizabeth didn't own a poodle skirt, but she put her hair into a ponytail.

Simpler times, here I come!

Jessica leaned against the wall next to the men's room door. "Be still, my heart," she said with a dramatic sigh, clasping a hand to her chest. "Oh, Izzy, did you ever see anything so scrumptious? I swear, I'd recognize my mystery man's back anywhere."

"There certainly is a lot of it," Isabella said. She had to struggle to keep a straight face. "A lot of his back, I mean."

"Did you see how he carries his shoulders? He's got to be six four, at least."

"Across the shoulders?" Isabella teased. "Must have been hard getting through that doorway."

Jessica swatted at her. "Don't make fun of me, Isabella. I think he may be the one."

Isabella raised her eyebrows in her patented gesture. "Jess, you're making me a little nervous."

"I know, I know, nobody trusts me not to mess up my life again. But this guy couldn't be less like Mike McAllery."

"You can tell that from looking at his back?"

"He saved my life, Izzy! More than once! I just know he's a nice guy." Jessica's mouth tightened. "Unlike Tom Watts."

"Is Elizabeth still upset?" Isabella asked.

"Upset? Are you kidding? She's like a zombie."

Just what Isabella hadn't wanted to hear! "They're such a great couple," she said. "I wish we'd never come on this cruise."

"Anyway, it's probably a good thing that she found out the truth about Tom before things

94

went any further between them. So how did Jason take the news?"

"What do you mean?" Isabella asked in alarm.

"Didn't Danny tell him?"

"He better not have!"

"How can you say that?" Jessica swung her long blond hair defiantly. "Danny's his best man. He has to tell him. That's what friends are for. If I'd listened to my friends about Mike, I would have been a lot better off. And so would he."

Isabella put an arm around Jessica. "I'm sorry you had to suffer the way you did, Jess. You really didn't deserve it. And I'm sorry Liz is so down. But breaking up Jason and Nicole isn't going to make anyone feel better."

"If I saw Danny kissing another girl, you mean you wouldn't want me to tell you?"

"No, thanks!" Isabella said. "If it's a serious kiss, I'm going to find out anyway because he's going to leave me for her. And if it's not serious, why should I lose any sleep over it?"

"Isabella Ricci, I'm shocked! You mean I can't count on you to tell me if he cheats on me?" Jessica put a reverent hand on the men's-room door.

Isabella sighed impatiently. She had work to do on her own, *real* relationship with Danny. She didn't have time to get sucked into one of Jessica's fantasies.

"I'm not interested in being a kiss cop," she said, bristling. "Anyway, your guy seems more inclined to hang around men's rooms than to kiss girls."

Jessica glared at Isabella and yanked open the door.

"Jess, are you crazy? Close that door!" Isabella pulled at her friend's arm. "I was only kidding, for pete's sake."

Jessica ignored her. "Hello! Anyone in there?"

No answer came from the white-tiled room.

"Hello?" she tried again. "Anyone home? Fair warning, I'm coming in on the count of three. One . . . two . . . three."

As Isabella watched, aghast, Jessica walked into the men's room. The door closed behind her.

"Shoot!" Jessica called out a minute later. "There's another door, into the barbershop. He escaped! And it's all your fault, Isabella!"

At first the dinghy trip seemed like prime adventure, the craft's single sail responding almost magically to Denise's confident handling.

Then the wind whipped up and the salt spray stuck to her hot skin, and once or twice she caught Winston looking nervous. All in all, she was limp with relief when land came into view.

Winston jumped out, yanked the small boat up onto the sand, and knotted the rope to a weathered mooring post. "Terra firma!" he cried ecstatically, flinging himself facedown on the sand. "I never thought to embrace you again."

Denise jumped down from the boat. She nudged Winston's leg with her foot. "If you get your lips all covered with sand, it's the last embrace you'll have," she warned.

Then she flopped next to him and let out a groan of relief. "Winnie, I hereby renounce all my aspirations to become a mermaid," she said. "It's big out there."

"I manfully swallowed my panic," Winston said. "But it kept looking to me as if the horizon were getting farther away. I'm still not sure we hit the right island."

"Of course we did," Denise said. "Didn't we? I mean, we went the way the guy pointed. It's got to be the right island. Because if it's not—"

"—it's the wrong island," Winston said. "And that would be—"

"—unthinkable," Denise finished. She closed her eyes and surrendered to the heavenly feeling of stability.

"What are you writing?" she asked moments later, aware of Winston moving a stick through the white sand.

"I'm not writing, I'm uncovering something," he said. "Oh, look, it's a sign."

Denise looked. Winston had drawn a big

square and written WRIGHT ISLAND in the middle of it. She kicked him again, and then she giggled. They rolled around in the warm sand, and Denise giggled some more. "Any island is the right island as long as you're on it," she said, settling into his arms.

"Sometimes you sound amazingly like a woman in love," Winston responded.

She faked alarm. "Is that true? My goodness, I'd better watch it. Because if he ever finds out—"

"If who finds out?" Winston asked.

"The man I love—" she said.

"If he finds out what?"

"That I'm in love with him—"

"Then what?" Winston demanded.

"Then he might get smug. And not be lovable. So I can't let him know."

"It'll be our secret," Winston said.

"Promise?"

"Cross my heart," he said, and kissed her.

"Winston, a serious thought just crossed my sun-poisoned brain," she said a few minutes later. "It's about our friend Bryan."

"Bryan who?" Winston said lazily.

She kicked him a third time. "Don't be bad, Winston. You owe the guy a favor. We've got to get ourselves to the airport and send for him. You and I have each other, but he's all alone over there." She waved vaguely out toward the sea.

"Are you kidding? By now he's probably organized a revolutionary army. I'm sure there's something to demonstrate against on that island."

"The quality of the fleet," Denise said. She sat up and surveyed the blank expanse of beach and rocks. "Speaking of which, is it okay to leave the *Jeanne d'Arc* just tied up like that? I thought there would be more of a harbor."

"Joan of Arc is supposed to be tied to a stake," Winston said, swinging his legs out of range of a fourth kick. Then he looked around. "Maybe the harbor's on the other side of the island. But I don't want to set off again, do you? It's going to be dark pretty soon. I'd rather take a chance on leaving the boat. I have a feeling we're much better off walking. There seems to be some sort of path up the rocks over there." He pointed.

Denise patted the prow of the dinghy. "Don't go anywhere without us," she said.

They started climbing.

The Soda Fountain looked exactly as advertised: it had a long bar with milk-shake machines whirring away behind it, a jukebox playing "Rock Around the Clock," a peppy wait staff with red-and-white-striped shirts, and lots of little tables with heart-shaped wrought-iron chairs. Unfortunately the brochure had failed to mention that Elizabeth would see Todd Wilkins and Gin-Yung

99

Suh sitting in two of those chairs. They were giggling over a soda, in a scene straight from an old Archie comic.

Todd and Gin-Yung were sharing one tall glass with two straws. The picture of teen contentment. And Gin-Yung didn't have to fake it to get that fifties look: a short, peppy haircut, an oversize man's button-down shirt, and penny loafers were her everyday getup.

Elizabeth tried to back out of the door before she was spotted, but too late. Todd was waving her over, the friendliest he'd been in ages.

Forcing a smile, she sat down at their table.

"Isn't this the greatest?" Todd said expansively. He put his arm around Gin-Yung's shoulders. "Liz, this cruise is one of the best things that's ever happened to me. And I'm sure you're having as awesome a time as I am."

Elizabeth nodded with all the enthusiasm she could muster, but her stomach was clenching. *Oh no*, she thought. *Todd thinks Tom and I are still a couple*.

A day ago she would have been genuinely happy to see Todd with a new love in his life. Her ex-boyfriend's college career had gotten off on the wrongest-possible foot—an affair with clingy, superficial Lauren Hill and then an athletic scandal in which he had been a scapegoat. Gin-Yung definitely represented a step in a better direction.

Although Elizabeth didn't know her well, she liked what she knew. Gin-Yung obviously had her own identity—the opposite of Lauren. And she didn't seem the sort to run away if Todd hit trouble again.

"Maybe the four of us can have some fun together," Todd said cheerfully. "Have you checked out the bowling alley? Of course, you'll have to put up with some competition from the athlete here—she considers any game under two-eighty not worth talking about."

"I could use some fun," Elizabeth said shakily. "Tom and I are finished," she blurted.

Todd's eyes popped. "Liz, you're kidding!"

"Wish I were," she said miserably.

"But I thought you guys were—"

"—the Rock of Gibraltar," Elizabeth chimed in with a rueful smile. "Well, it crumbled."

"I'm sorry, Elizabeth," Gin-Yung said.

Elizabeth could see that the other girl meant the sympathetic words—but felt uncomfortable, too. "I'm the one who should be sorry," Elizabeth said. "You guys came in here for fun, and now I've spoiled it. I think I'll take my rain cloud back to the cabin."

"No, you don't," Todd said, putting a firm hand on her chair as she started to push it back. "We're going to cheer you up." He waved at the waitress. "Does a brown cow sound good?"

"What's that?"

"Root beer with vanilla ice cream. It's what we're having."

Elizabeth started to protest, but he went ahead and ordered for her. She had to admit that a glass full of ice cream sounded awfully good.

"So what happened?" Todd asked gently. "Do you want to talk about it?"

"It's the last thing I want to talk about," Elizabeth said. But Todd was looking at her so compassionately, and he seemed so wonderfully familiar in this alien setting, that she promptly spilled out the whole saga.

"I suppose you think I'm overreacting," she finished. "I know that's what everyone's going to tell me. One kiss—big deal."

He patted her hand. "If you were anybody else, I might think you were overreacting. But it's you, Liz. Nobody's as loyal as you are. So I guess it's not surprising that you expect the same thing in return. Anyway," he went on, "you actually saw it. Maybe if you'd just heard about it, you wouldn't be so blown away. But to see it—wow! That must have been the worst."

His unexpected warmth was as delicious and soothing as the soda that the waitress put in front of her. She began to cry—this time out of relief.

As Elizabeth looked up to thank Todd, she saw

through her blur that Gin-Yung had gotten to her feet.

"Thank you for the soda, Todd," Gin-Yung said stiffly. "But I seem to have lost my appetite. So if you two will excuse me, I'll leave you to your nostalgia while I get back to the nineties."

Chapter Eight

Denise emerged from the deserted trail she and Winston had followed from the beach. Picking up her pace, she hurried toward the hotel just ahead, already anticipating their rescue. At the foot of an overgrown path, they both stopped in their tracks.

Winston and Denise stared at the dilapidated building, shaking their heads at the huge sign reading PLEASURE PALACE. The hotel's gray facade looked as though it hadn't been washed in decades, and sections of the huge front porch sagged almost to the ground.

"Pleasure Palace," Winston said aloud. "This just goes to prove that you can't believe everything you read. Especially when it's written on a rotting wooden sign."

"Morbid Motel would be more like it," Denise said, nodding.

"How about Lots-of-Luck Lodge?" Winston suggested.

"Or Lots of Lice," Denise said wryly.

As unappealing as the run-down, desolate inn was, Winston pointed out that it boasted one distinct virtue—it was there. And the next morning, when the cruise ship came, they could put Pleasure Palace behind them forever.

According to the faded magazine story framed in the lobby, Pleasure Palace was the sole commercial establishment on the island. Once the private estate of a famous playboy, it had also been a resort for a brief time. For the past several years it had apparently been languishing in search of a new owner.

"I don't understand why someone keeps this place open at all," Denise said, surveying the dusty, ghostly expanse. "We seem to be the only guests in this half of the century." They were literally the only people in sight, except for a skeleton staff.

"My guess is it's a tax write-off," Winston said. "We'll need things like that someday. Shall I buy it?"

"Why don't you buy me dinner instead?" Denise said.

Winston turned to one of the few staff members. The man sat next to a fan, reading a newspaper. "Excuse me, sir? Who do we see about ordering some dinner in this fine establishment?"

The man glanced up from his newspaper. "You've got two choices, kid. Frozen pizza or microwave hot dogs."

Winston looked at Denise. "Maybe we should try to get a helicopter right away, Win," she whispered.

Winston took a few steps closer to the man he'd been talking to. "Maybe we'll skip dinner and head to the airstrip," he said. "Can you tell us how we can hire a helicopter?"

The man looked at Winston as if he were a petulant child. "Airstrip? Helicopter? We haven't had an airstrip here since the last of the jet-setters took their good time to Hawaii."

Denise shook her head slowly. She could live on frozen pizza and microwave hot dogs until the *Homecoming Queen* docked. *But what are we going to do about Bryan?* she wondered miserably.

Bryan sat on the beach, staring glumly at the magnificent sunset. The vibrant shades of orange, red, and purple made him miss Nina, who had a special passion for sunsets. And they made him hungry. If Nina were there, she'd be extolling the swaths of apricot, the streaks of grape, the hints of lime. She always talked about sunsets as if a painter had dipped brushes in fruit juice and then smeared them across the sky.

Bryan bit his lip, imagining how good a grape would taste at the moment. Even a spoonful of grape jelly would have been welcome. Grape jelly and a mound of cream cheese on a bagel would have been absolute bliss.

He tried to think about Ghandi, fasting for days or weeks at a time, hoping to prick the conscience of mankind. But it was one thing to starve on principle and quite another to be starved by a quirk of fate.

As the sun slid toward the west, the temperature dropped. Bryan knew he should move up off the beach, but the nearer he got to the shops and restaurants above the harbor, the more frustrated he became. At least down on the beach he couldn't smell conch fritters and the tangy aroma of luscious jerk chicken.

Jerk chicken! He laughed ruefully. The Caribbean delicacy could be his nickname. He'd been a jerk to blow up at Nina for going parasailing with Dr. Daniels. In fact, he'd been a jerk about Nina and a lot of things. And despite Denise and Winston's assurance that everyone had personal phobias, he regarded himself as a hundred percent chicken when it came to water.

Bryan could barely stand to think about his two classmates in that walnut shell of a boat, bobbing around on the crashing surf. He prayed that Denise was playing captain; if Winston was at the helm, they were likely to end up in Hudson Bay. Until Bryan saw the flash of a helicopter propeller in the sky, he would have terrifying doubts about their safety—as well as his own.

Suddenly Bryan heard a sound behind him.

"Pardon, monsieur—" a male voice said.

The muscles in Bryan's shoulders tensed. Adrenaline coursed through his body. On top of everything else that had happened, was he about to be mugged on the deserted beach? Of course, he had nothing to hand over. "Sorry. I gave at the souvenir stand," Bryan could imagine himself saying to the mugger.

What would the guy take from him instead of money—his life?

Jessica looked from the cabin's small closet to Elizabeth. "Liz, where's that green washed-silk dress?"

"You mean *my* green washed-silk dress? Way over on the right, I think," Elizabeth said.

"I don't see it," Jessica said a moment later. "I wish you'd keep better track of your wardrobe."

Elizabeth rolled her eyes and tried to lose herself in the crossword puzzle she was doing. Appropriately enough, the puzzle was called Double or Nothing, and many of the long clues were about things or phrases that came in pairs. Bacon and eggs. Horse and carriage. His and hers.

Jessica slammed the nice wooden hangers into each other, then headed to the dresser. "Maybe the dress got mixed up with our nightgowns," she said. "We unpacked really fast." She rummaged around the drawers, throwing several nightgowns on the floor.

"Oops." With a guilty start, Elizabeth remembered that she hadn't packed the dress. "Sorry, Jess. I didn't bring it. It has a stain on it." Knowing what was coming, she put down her pencil and clapped her hands over her ears.

"A what? A stain? Why didn't you take it to the cleaners? You know how I feel about that dress." Jessica's voice rose higher and higher. "Sometimes you're just so self-centered."

Elizabeth waited until the storm had died down. "It's my dress," she said quietly. "And you packed more clothes than all the rest of us put together. Why don't you wear, um, that new black-and-white thing? It'll show off your tan."

Jessica glanced at the dozen dresses she'd packed. "I guess I *did* bring a lot," she conceded. "Okay," she said grudgingly. She took the dress off its hanger. "What are you wearing to dinner?"

"Haven't decided," Elizabeth said. She filled in the last big clue of the crossword puzzle—night and day. "I think I'll take a little nap first and then a long, cool shower. So you go ahead."

"Well, don't be late," Jessica said. "I've got a

plan to trap my mystery man, and I need your help."

Elizabeth groaned. Just what she needed—one of Jessica's plans. "What am I supposed to do?" she asked dryly. "Pretend to be you? Then when I fall overboard and he dives into the water to rescue me, you dive in and snag him?"

"Liz, that's brilliant!" Jessica exclaimed, her blue-green eyes widening in admiration. "I couldn't have thought of a better plan myself. Would you?"

"Jessica Wakefield, I was joking!" Elizabeth replied emphatically. "Don't even think about it! Besides, I could use a little rescuing myself at the moment. Now please finish dressing so I can have a nap."

Elizabeth pulled a blanket around her, closed her eyes, and almost immediately fell into a deep sleep. Minutes later, she was dreaming.

She was on a ship, but something was terribly wrong. In fact, everything was wrong. The ship was going too fast, crazily fast, like a runaway van with the brakes cut.

She was up on deck with Danny, trying to breathe, when the captain came up behind them. Peeling off his mask, he revealed the terrifying truth. He wasn't good Captain Avedon. He was William White.

"Read the fine print," he sneered.

111

"What does he mean?" she frantically asked Danny. But Danny just shrugged.

William laughed menacingly as the ship raced even faster. "It's all in the name," he said, folding his arms across his chest. "You used to be so smart," he taunted Elizabeth. "Or was Tom Watts always the real brain?"

"Tom's history," Danny said.

"Well, Elizabeth's flunking history this semester," William returned. "You're all flunking history. Because unless you figure out the clue, you're dead." He pulled on a lifejacket as the ship swayed from side to side.

Suddenly Elizabeth had an idea. In a desperate move that took her last ounce of courage, she ran to the railing and peered over the side. The name of the ship was painted in bold black letters on the prow. Peering at it, she saw the fine print that William had been talking about.

Her heart nearly exploded with terror. The SS in the *Homecoming Queen*'s name stood for secret society!

They were all going to die—and she was the one who had bought the tickets for the cruise.

Her eyes flew open. She put one hand against her throat in an effort to calm the wild pulsing. What a dream!

It wasn't surprising that she was still having nightmares. The events of her freshman year had

112

given her unconscious enough raw material to fuel any number of nightmares.

She'd almost fallen in love with starkly handsome and brilliant William, only to discover that he was the mastermind behind the secret society terrorizing the campus. Then she'd survived an attempt on her life only to come within inches of taking all her friends down with her, when William had lured them onto a van with cut brakes. Todd had saved their lives by coming up with the idea of steering the truck uphill to slow its momentum enough to let them roll off. But all of them had been slower to heal in spirit than in body.

Even after William himself had died, the weird twists had continued. He'd left her all his money, and his family's efforts to contest the will had failed. Maybe, Elizabeth thought now, she should have followed her original impulse—to give all the money to charity.

She'd decided at the last minute that it made sense for William to buy some pleasure for the people he'd tried to kill. After all, it was entirely his fault that they all needed this vacation as they'd never needed one before.

Shivering, Elizabeth couldn't suppress the awful notion that William had somehow jinxed this cruise.

"No!" she said aloud. She refused to allow William White to cause her any more pain.

William hadn't defeated her in life, and she wasn't about to let him defeat her in death.

As she headed for the shower Elizabeth made up her mind that she was going to enjoy the rest of her vacation. And she was going to help everyone else enjoy it, too. *Everyone but Tom,* she added to herself. *I hope he gets a permanent case of seasickness!*

Chapter
Nine

"*Bonjour.* Good morning. Time to wake up."

As the voice filtered through layers of sleep, Bryan opened his eyes to near total darkness. *Where am I?* he thought, with a flutter of panic.

"Did you sleep well?" the voice asked.

Rubbing his eyes, Bryan managed to focus on the face grinning down at him. Details of the previous evening came rushing back.

The man on the beach hadn't been a mugger—quite the opposite. He was a native fisherman named Jean Martin, and he'd possibly saved Bryan's life. He'd brought Bryan back to his cozy little house near the harbor. Then he'd given him two bowls of delicious conch stew for dinner, as well as a sofa to sleep on. In exchange, Bryan had promised to work with him today.

Now Jean was handing Bryan a mug of

steaming café au lait. "There's fresh bread to go with it when you get yourself to the table," Jean said. "But hurry. The fish don't wait."

The table had been roughly constructed out of driftwood. And although the chairs were hard and uncomfortable, Bryan felt as though he were sitting in the lap of luxury. The vista of ocean and early-morning sky was magnificent.

Sitting down, Bryan followed his rescuer's example and dunked chunks of the bread into the coffee. The simple meal tasted delicious.

Who needs cappuccino and croissants at some glitzy café? he thought. *I've never had a better breakfast.*

As he stared out at the misty predawn gray, contentment seeped into every cell in his body.

He looked at Jean Martin and mentally compared the two of them. They were about the same age. They were the same height, had similar shades of skin, and probably weighed within five pounds of each other—although the fisherman looked like his weight consisted entirely of muscle.

But this guy is happier than I'll ever be, Bryan thought. Jean had to boil his water on a rustic hot plate, but he seemed to be in tune with himself and nature. *What he's got, nobody can pick-pocket.*

Bryan took a last swallow of the rich coffee.

116

"Put me to work," he said to Jean. "I'm ready."

Humming, he followed his new friend into the fresh morning air.

Then he saw the boat.

Jessica surveyed the line at the breakfast buffet. She'd never seen so many short guys in one place. Well, not exactly short, but anyone under six four fit her current definition of the word.

She had thought this would be the perfect place to trap Mr. Mystery. She was convinced that if she saw him in the light of day, she'd somehow recognize him instantly. Forcing herself out of bed in case he was an early riser, she'd been waiting in front of the double doors, inhaling coffee and bacon aromas, when the steward had unlocked the dining room at seven.

It was now a quarter past eight, and the good news was that her guardian angel wasn't inclined to get up at the crack of dawn. The bad news was that she had breakfast coming out of her ears. The only way she could justify keeping her table was by going through the line every half hour or so and getting at least a token of food on her plate.

"Back again?" a waitress said, tiredly plopping neon yellow scrambled eggs on Jessica's plate. "How do you keep your figure?"

"I'm going to spend the whole day working

117

out," Jessica lied cheerfully. *And I'm going to put these eggs into my napkin.*

She went back to her table, looking at the breakfast food with as much enthusiasm as she could muster. With a fork in one hand, she pretended to read the novel she'd brought along for cover. But her eyes stayed glued to the buffet line. Spotting some cute guys in California State sweatshirts, she made a halfhearted attempt to fall in love with them. But it was no use.

I just have to keep on waiting, she said to herself. *He's bound to show up eventually.*

"You know, I'm taking this best-man business very seriously," Danny said.

"You're not kidding," Jason replied. He poured maple syrup over his French toast. "Sometimes I wish you were just my better man." He took a bite of his breakfast, chewing thoughtfully. "Do you like Nicole?" he asked suddenly.

The blunt question floored Danny. "Sure I do. What's not to like about her?" *Aside from her having kissed my best friend,* he added silently.

"Sometimes I feel like you're trying to break us up," Jason said, his tone serious.

"Who, me?" Danny asked, feigning astonishment. "That's crazy!" He hastily gulped cold milk to counteract the sweat breaking out on his forehead. He desperately needed to push the conversation in a different direction.

"Actually, on the way to the breakfast I stopped in at the ship's library to get some ideas for my toast. Not toast as in French toast—the toast I'll make at the wedding." Danny fought back the urge to laugh hysterically.

"You did? Hey, that's great," Jason said.

"I thought I could build it around this idea the Victorians had. They used to make anagrams of a man and woman's name to see what fate had in store for them."

"You mean, like combine the letters in Nicole and Jason?"

"Exactly," Danny said. "But I hate to tell you, Jason—" Sighing massively, he took a pen from his pocket and wrote NICOLEJASON across the top of a paper napkin. "Look at the words you can make with those letters." He pointed them out with his pen. "Jail. Saloon. Both loco and insane. I don't know how to say this, but I even found loose." He darted a glance around the room to make sure Isabella wasn't approaching. "That could mean . . . fooling around."

"I know what loose means," Jason snapped. "Well, I look at our names together and I see son." He glared at Danny. "You're talking about the mother of my future children."

Danny thought quickly. "You don't need the

letters in Nicole to have a son, Jason. It's right there in your own name."

"Danny, just what are you trying to accomplish?"

"Nothing, man. Nothing."

Jason pushed back his plate of half-eaten food and searched Danny's face. He nodded knowingly. "You know what I think? It's not that you don't like Nicole. It's the opposite, isn't it? Tell me the truth, Danny." He looked into Danny's eyes. "Are you in love with my fiancée?"

Danny almost fainted. "Jason, no; you've got it all wrong. I—I—"

"You what?"

I've never been less in love with anybody. "I'm only in love with Isabella," Danny managed to say. "Please don't get me in trouble with her. She's really possessive," he lied.

"Well, if you don't dislike Nicole and you're not in love with her, you have no excuse. So start acting like a real best man, or you're fired!"

Elizabeth had a sixth sense that let her know when Jessica wanted company and when she wanted to be alone. This was definitely one of the latter times.

No, she contradicted herself, as she got into line at the sumptuous breakfast buffet, *not alone.* Her twin had an anticipatory air about her. But the company she was waiting for wasn't a sister's. Jessica just wanted to be alone until *he* came along.

The *he* of the moment was the guy she kept calling her mystery man, and Elizabeth wasn't sure whether the guy was real or imaginary or something in between. Probably Jessica would spend her whole life with one foot grounded in reality and the other walking on air.

It occurred to Elizabeth that in a weird way Jessica was the true—if not the technical—innocent. Each day life started over for Jessica, as if neither she nor the world had any history. She didn't always learn everything she should from her experiences, but she wasn't jaded by them, either. She was eternally full of hope.

I envy her, Elizabeth realized abruptly, startling herself. People assumed that Elizabeth was the sensible twin, but maybe that wasn't true. Maybe there was some sort of wisdom in taking life as it came.

And maybe Todd was more like Jessica than Elizabeth had ever realized. She thought back to the sports scandal. It was innocence more than corruption that had led Todd to accept illegal gifts from the administration. True, he'd gotten really full of himself for a while. But he'd paid a big price—he'd been suspended from the team and had temporarily become a social outcast. But unlike Jessica, he seemed to have learned from his mistakes.

Now he was really trying to get his act together. Maybe he and Elizabeth should try to get their act together again too. Was it too late?

"I don't mean to get personal, but are you sure you're not eating for two?"

At the sound of the voice from the other side of the buffet table, Elizabeth was brought back to the present.

"Pardon me?" she said politely to the waitress who was addressing her.

The other woman was spooning out scrambled eggs. "I know the chef makes great eggs, but I didn't know they were this great. Here, think this will hold you?" She upended the serving pan and heaped the entire contents onto Elizabeth's plate.

The twins had dressed similarly that morning, in nautical striped T-shirts and white jeans. Elizabeth quickly realized that the waitress thought she was Jessica. Well, let her think what she wanted after her embarrassing comment.

"I never eat eggs," she announced, taking a small measure of satisfaction as confusion crept across the woman's face. Instantly she wished she had bitten her tongue. If Tom were there, she would have been much more polite. But if Tom were there, she wouldn't be in such a bad mood.

"Who says you don't eat eggs?" Todd asked behind her.

She almost dropped the laden plate. "I was just thinking about you," she murmured.

"You're blushing!" he said, looking amazed.

"Well, I should be," she said. "I was rude to that hardworking waitress. Worse, I enjoyed it."

"How humane of you, Elizabeth," Todd said drily. "And I think a blush suits you nicely."

"Maybe it does," she said pertly. *And maybe flirting does too,* she added inwardly.

She batted her eyelashes. "Want to join me for breakfast?"

Tom Watts was no stranger to guilt. He'd found plenty of reason to hate himself in the past. But he'd thought those days were over. Guilt was about the old Tom Watts, the self-involved jock who lived for the thrill of the moment. The new Tom Watts—the sensitive, caring crusader with whom Elizabeth had fallen in love—wasn't prey to such feelings.

He was a good guy now, and a good guy should be able to look at himself in the mirror without fear and loathing.

But Tom looked into the mirror and saw troubled eyes surrounded with rings of sleeplessness. He saw a bruised chin, where Danny's fist had connected; the inflamed redness was a neon sign proclaiming his fall from grace.

The sight of his face was so upsetting that he

123

decided to keep his distance from the breakfast buffet. His friends apparently felt the same way about him that he did, so why spoil everyone's appetite?

The one person who was still treating him like a member of the human race was Jason Pierce, ironically enough. He must still be in the dark about the kiss Tom and Nicole shared. *Thank heaven for small favors.*

Eager to avoid the crowd, Tom headed in the opposite direction from the buffet. Moments later he found himself on the Siesta deck. *Of course. The villain always returns to the scene of the crime.*

As if drawn by some dark inner compulsion, he traced his footsteps to the exact spot where he had kissed Nicole. Closing his eyes, he relived the forbidden sweetness of the kiss. Then he opened his eyes and visualized the look of abject misery on Elizabeth's face. He felt the force of Danny's blow.

Rubbing his chin, his mood swiveled from guilt to anger. He'd made a huge mistake—but he'd paid his dues. The hurt in Elizabeth's eyes would have been punishment enough, even without Danny's follow-up punch. So he'd been weak enough to kiss his old girlfriend, and dumb enough to do it where he could be spotted. Did that mean he deserved to be tortured forever?

At that moment Tom would have given anything to be Shelley or Keats. If only he could express his love for Elizabeth in a poem so passionate that she would forgive him totally. And then they could go back to where they had been before this trip had started—deeply in love, full of possibility.

Leaning against the railing, Tom tried to make a poem happen. Unfortunately his mind was completely blank. And maybe a poem would be subject to misunderstanding anyway, like the roommate business had been. He couldn't risk getting it wrong again.

He made up his mind. He was going to head for the dining room and confront her. He'd throw himself literally at her feet if he had to.

Smoothing the hair that the wind had tousled, he turned away from the railing. *By now she's probably started to miss me,* he assured himself. She was probably sitting alone at a table with a book, secretly hoping he'd show up and apologize.

Well, ready or not, here I come.

Todd hid his confusion behind his coffee cup. He felt as if he were in a dream.

An intimate breakfast with Elizabeth had been one of the abiding fantasies of their high school years, central to his image of the future. He'd pictured honeymoon breakfasts in bed, Elizabeth in a peach silk nightgown and one perfect rose on the tray. He'd imagined old-married breakfasts in the kitchen. "Honey, pass me the sports section, will you?"

They'd often had breakfast together last fall, when they'd first gotten to SVU, but it had never been the morning-after-the-night-before breakfast of his fantasies. Elizabeth might not have believed it, but breakfast had been on his mind when he'd tried to talk her into bed last fall. Sure, he'd wanted to make love to her. But he'd also wanted what came after—talk, tenderness, and orange juice for two.

The orange juice was there now, all right. And the talk was flowing. As for tenderness—how else could he read the gentle smile that played at the corners of her mouth?

"You certainly look a lot happier than you did yesterday," he said.

"I am. Thank you so much for letting me unload on you. I'm sorry if I ruined your date." She paused expectantly.

His mind raced. He knew what he was supposed to say. *It doesn't matter, Liz, because Gin-Yung doesn't matter.*

But he couldn't say what Elizabeth wanted to hear, because Gin-Yung did matter. He didn't know her very well, but he knew her enough to want to know more. She was definitely special.

But so was Elizabeth Wakefield. And suddenly he wanted to know more about her, too—as she was now. There had been a time when he could practically read her mind. And maybe the closeness they'd once shared still lingered.

"It's okay, Elizabeth," he finally said. "Gin-Yung's pretty understanding. She's a lot like you that way. In fact," he continued, "she's a lot like you, period."

"I take that as a compliment," Elizabeth responded.

"You should." Todd's voice was almost a whisper.

The sound of forks and knives against the ship's blue-and-white china was almost deafening in the silence that suddenly descended. Todd could hear his thoughts pounding against his brain, and his head was starting to ache. Confusion over Elizabeth and Gin-Yung was descending over him like a thick fog, and he had no idea what he was going to do.

As Nicole nibbled on a blueberry muffin she flipped the pages of *Veil,* a magazine for brides. One article was called "How to Keep the Honeymoon Glow Forever." Another purported to have the answer to that age-old question, "What Do the Holes in Your Husband's Socks Tell You about Him?"

Sometimes the word *husband* looked very peculiar to Nicole. A husband was what her mother had. A husband was for a woman who wore suits, made piecrusts from scratch, and got respect from traffic cops. None of the above applied to her.

Although she had a responsible job in a major law firm lined up for the summer, the position was very junior. The partners would all be "Mr. So-and-So" and "Ms. Such-and-Such." And she would be Nicole, which was fine with her.

People kept asking her whether she was going to keep her last name or become Mrs. Pierce or play around with hyphens. She couldn't decide any more than she could pick out a serious china pattern, because it felt too ridiculously unreal.

As for what she would name her first child—the article she'd just turned to was titled "Ten Names NOT to Give Your First Child"—that seemed eons away. There was so much to think about before she dealt with kids' names—whether to go to law school, for instance.

At first she'd been walking on air when Jason had proposed. They'd been in love for years, and she was positive that they were meant to be together. But for the last few weeks Jason had seemed to be pulling away. Was it just typical last-minute jitters? Or was he no longer in love with her? She couldn't hold back the flood of doubts. *Is Jason really ready for marriage?*

And even more to point, was she? She'd thought so. But seeing Tom had thrown her off balance. It wasn't that she was in love with Tom, or ever had been. But seeing a guy she used to date had reminded her that there were other relationships out there. Was she making the right choice with Jason? After all, marriage was forever.

Looking down at the magazine, she saw that she had turned to an article with a bold purple headline: "A Survival Guide to Broken Engagements (Yes, Virginia, You Will Smile Again)."

She angrily slapped the magazine shut.

Tom paused outside the dining room and re-rolled the sleeves of the plaid shirt he wore open over a T-shirt. He couldn't decide if it would be easier if Elizabeth were alone or sitting with a bunch of her friends. Isabella, at least, might show some pity for Tom and encourage Elizabeth to talk to him. Then again, she might tell Tom he was scum and throw a glass of orange juice in his face. And Jessica could always be counted on to go on the offensive when she thought someone was trying to hurt her sister. Tom tried not to imagine the scathing remarks Jessica was capable of hurling at him.

And what he had to say was pretty private. So maybe it would be better if she were alone. He sighed. There was no point to standing in the corridor, wondering and wishing. He had to go into the dining room and apologize.

As he searched the crowded, noisy room for Elizabeth's shining hair, his gaze suddenly stopped cold. He stood, paralyzed, staring at the one sight he hadn't considered—Elizabeth and Todd Wilkins, their heads close together.

Tom closed his eyes. *I'm hallucinating,* he said to himself. *This is just a nightmare.* He forced himself to open his eyes again.

And then he faced the truth. The nightmare was real.

Dr. Daniels made a face as he bit into his jam-covered English muffin. "I wish they'd get real crumpets," he complained. "You know, of course, that there's no such thing as an English muffin in England. I learned my lesson about that the summer I spent at Oxford."

"Oh, really," Nina said.

"And there's no French toast in France, or Danish pastry in Denmark. And do you know what happened when I ordered a hamburger *à l'américain* during a ski trip to Megève?"

"I can't imagine, Richard." Nina stifled a yawn.

"The hamburger came out with a fried egg on top! Which is only part of the reason why I prefer to ski Gstaad now. Of course, my family keeps a condo in Aspen, because sometimes it's impossible for any of us to get away for more than a long weekend."

"Life is rough," Nina commented.

"It's great being able just to pop over to Aspen by plane, but one of these days I'm going to drive the Beamer from Miami to Aspen and see how the other half lives."

"Beamer?"

Richard gave her the look of a teacher whose prize student has unexpectedly slipped. "I told you that I drive a BMW," he said.

"Oh, yeah, sure," Nina said. "I just forgot its first name."

"And you keep forgetting mine," he said. "It's Rich to my close friends."

If Bryan had been there, he would have told Rich how many inner-city kids he could feed for a month if he sold his beloved Beamer. *And I'd be mad at Bryan*, she had to admit to herself. *But proud, too.*

Richard looked at his watch. "It's nine o'Rolex," he said. "We'll be docking at Juma in an hour or so. Want to hit the duty-free shops with me?"

"Don't you already have everything you need?" Nina asked gently. She put down her coffee cup. "How many Beamers can a man wear? Uh, drive?"

"I know what you're saying, Nina. I had three years of analysis—with a disciple of Anna Freud's, it just so happens—so I've thought plenty on this subject." He paused. "The fact is, my inner child is still in need of constant attention. I will probably never have everything I need." He took her hand and looked into her eyes. "Unless I have you."

Nina took a deep breath. Richard had a tendency toward materialism and self-obsession, but at the moment he sounded sincere. Did he really love her?

She had started to find Richard wearing, but it felt good to have a guy completely intent on impressing her. Bryan never felt the need to tell her how much he cared.

Maybe life wasn't about Bryan's sexy voice and fiery passion for making the world a better place. It was possible that Nina would actually be better off with a rich doctor whose biggest worries in life were pleasing his girlfriend and making sure his inner child—whatever that was—felt like it was getting enough attention.

For the first time in ages, Nina would have welcomed her mother's advice.

She told Richard she wanted to go back to her cabin and write a letter. And maybe on the shopping.

Maybe on everything.

Corned-beef hash had sounded like a good

idea, but Bruce was unable to eat more than a few forkfuls. Lila wasn't at the buffet—La Contessa had no doubt ordered cabin service. But in spirit she sat across from him.

"Such plebeian food," she would probably tease.

"I felt like slumming," he would probably tease back.

Then they would trade satisfied glances across the table, two rich kids who were comfortable with their circumstances and with each other.

The absence of stress over money was just one of the many great characteristics of their relationship. They liked the same music, they needed about the same amount of sleep, and there were lots of parallels between their families. Plus, when they danced, she fitted into his arms as though she'd been made to measure.

Aside from all the superficial qualities they shared, Bruce and Lila had a deep-down respect for each other. It had been forged in the Sierra Nevada, when they had pulled each other through subzero cold and life-threatening wounds. Underneath the fluff, Lila was made of iron, and she'd seen that he was more than an immature spoiled brat.

I can't believe she's going to turn her back on me, he thought. They'd had to skirt the edge of death to find out how much they cared for each other.

133

How could she even consider wasting that precious knowledge?

She can't, he decided. He broke off a piece of toast and bit determinedly into it. He wouldn't let her. They were made for each other.

Maybe it was too soon for her to be in love, but in love was what she was. They'd both thrown away so much in their lives. Bruce refused to be discarded like last season's outfit, no matter what Lila's pigheaded brother-in-law had to say about it.

"Leonardo, stop!" Alex said, in a far corner of the cavernous dining room. "You're just teasing me."

"Oh, but I'm not, Signorina Alexandra. I think you must be part Italian. I can see it in your beautiful eyes."

"But all the branches on my family tree are English, Scottish, and a touch of Finnish," Alex said.

Leonardo raised his dark eyebrows. "Maybe one of those branches got involved with a twig that no one has told you about," he suggested. "But it doesn't really matter, does it?" He cupped his café au lait and took a long, meaningful sip. "They say that beauty is its own reward. So perhaps it is also its own ancestor."

"I thought the saying is that virtue is its own reward," Alex commented.

"Oh?" he said innocently. "Well, that is certainly true. And probably its only reward." Putting down his cup, he slapped his own cheek. "But I mustn't talk in such a way to a young girl."

"I'm not so young," Alex shot back indignantly. "When I put my hair up, I can go to any bar without getting carded."

"Carded? That means drunk?"

She laughed nervously. "No, no. It means asked to show my ID card. To prove that I'm old enough to be served alcohol." What had made her bring up the loaded subject? She veered away from it. "It must be hard for you to understand all our expressions."

"Sometimes I do not understand the words, but then I listen to the eyes. The eyes say so much. Especially when they are as beautiful as yours, *bella* Alessandra."

She kindled at the Italian pronunciation of her name. She'd never been gladder about having changed it. Enid was just plain Enid in any language.

As Alex listened to Leonardo's extravagant compliments, the possibilities of life loomed as infinite. Especially if she figured out how to get things going again with Noah. She was acutely aware of him, a few tables away. She was enjoying Leonardo's charm, but she had to admit that she was mostly enjoying its possible impact on Noah.

She leaned across the table. "Your eyes are great too," she said to Leonardo. "So dark and deep."

"And can you hear what they are saying, Alessandra?"

Blushing crimson, she said, "I do believe I can."

And I hope Noah can too, she thought.

Noah could hardly believe his eyes. If Alex tilted forward any farther, she was going to land in Leonardo's coffee. What was she doing, auditioning for the Leaning Tower of Pisa look-alike contest?

He would have given anything to have her gaze at him with the eyes she was fixing on Leonardo's face. But how could he compete with someone that slick? Even before the handsome Italian had come into the picture, Noah had sometimes felt like a guy with two left feet—at least when he was around Alex.

For a while, he'd thought he was everything she needed. He'd been the one on whom she'd leaned. But it was a different kind of leaning from what she was doing with Leonardo.

Noah had been the helping hand she had needed to get back on her feet after she'd started drinking heavily and doing badly in all her classes. He had been a shoulder on which to rest her head while she sorted herself out.

He'd cheered her on as she'd gotten stronger and stronger, and she'd repaid his encouragement with a touching devotion. He'd been scrupulous, too, like the psychologist he was going to be someday. He'd never taken advantage of her dependence on him.

Slowly their relationship had evolved into something wonderful. In the past few weeks Noah had started to believe that Alex was truly in love with him.

When the spring break cruise had come up, he'd been ecstatic. The change of setting was just what they'd needed. Away from campus and their familiar hangouts, he could urge the relationship in a new direction. Against an exotic backdrop of turquoise seas, she might begin to look at him as something more than a healer.

As a lover, for instance.

Because he was in love with her. He loved her fragile beauty and her willingness to make mistakes and her insistence on defining herself: the whole Alex package.

He'd helped her fight her biggest battle, against the temptation of alcohol. He'd encouraged her to deal with the pressures of college life and decide what really mattered.

But where was his vaunted wisdom now that he needed it for himself? He was as awkward and shy as a child—so afraid of saying the wrong thing that sometimes he didn't say anything at all. He could almost imagine the two of them in the future, looking back on this time and laughing tenderly. *What kids we were! So in love with each other and not knowing how to say it!*

But Noah didn't know how to get them to that future. And Leonardo seemed to be driving a steamroller all over Noah's plans.

At the moment Noah would have cheerfully traded his legendary sensitivity for Leonardo's charm and Armani jacket. Unfortunately Leonardo didn't look the least bit inclined to trade.

Isabella wasn't sure whether or not she wanted to have breakfast with Danny, but she tugged her soft gray leggings straight just in case. Catching sight of him and Jason as she walked into the dining room, she instantly made up her mind. At the risk of wasting the perfect leggings, she didn't want to have breakfast with him. Not if Jason was on the menu.

She deliberately sat down at a big table of lively girls she'd met while playing miniature golf with Nicole.

The girls welcomed her warmly, but the distraction she'd sought wasn't there. Isabella might as well have sat in Danny's lap, she was so focused on him.

138

As the pleasant chatter rose and fell around her, she kept him firmly in her line of sight. She strained toward his table, trying to read every tilt of his head and wave of his hand.

He promised, she reminded herself. *He said he wouldn't tell.* And she was certain that he wouldn't break his promise to her, because that would be unethical.

But she suddenly wondered how ethical had she been to extract that promise. And what was it costing Danny to keep it? He'd been spending every minute with Jason. Asking him not to talk about that kiss was like leaving a chocoholic alone with a box of fudge. Even if he could resist, it must have been torturing him.

But she'd done it for his own good as well as the principle of the thing. If he blabbed to Jason, it could ruin their friendship. He'd wind up the cruise minus Jason as well as Tom.

"So, Isabella, who would you rather be marooned on an island with?" Olivia Ng was asking. "Keanu Reeves or Kevin Costner?"

Isabella tried to look amused by the question. But she wasn't in the mood for playing games. And the word *marooned* made her think about Denise and Winston. Were they okay?

Isabella adamantly wished that Elizabeth had never signed them up for this cruise. A week on the *Homecoming Queen* was looking less and less like a dream vacation. And more and more like William White's final act of revenge.

Jean Martin stared at Bryan. "You what?" he asked again.

"I can't get into that—thing," Bryan repeated miserably, looking away from the small boat.

The young fisherman was incredulous. "But why not?"

"It's too small," Bryan said, looking down. He kicked the wooden slats of the dock.

"I see," Jean stated coldly. He folded his arms across his chest. "My American friend only goes in yachts. My bread was good enough for him when he was starving, but my boat is not."

"Oh no!" Bryan cried, aghast. "It's—"

The islander cut him off. "I worked for two years to buy this boat. Do you even know the meaning of work, American? I gave you a place to sleep, I fed you two meals, and the deal was you work for me. Now get into that boat or—"

"I'm scared!" Bryan cried. "I'm scared, man! I'm a jerk chicken, okay? A chicken jerk. Say it any way you want. I can't get into your boat because I'm scared of the water."

Jean stared at him. "You're scared of the water and you went on a cruise?" he said skeptically.

"My girlfriend talked me into it. Anyway, it's not the same thing. The *Homecoming Queen*'s so

140

big, they could hold the World Cup in the ball-room. Look, I really do want to keep my end of the bargain. Can't I clean the fish when you bring them in? I don't care how smelly they are."

"And now you insult my fish!" Jean cried. "Fresh fish don't smell—didn't you know that?"

"No," Brian mumbled, despondent. Was it only a few brief minutes ago that he had experienced perfect bliss? "The only thing I do with water is drink it and shower in it. I don't swim in it. I don't—"

"Wait a minute. You don't swim?"

"My family couldn't afford a pool," Bryan said.

Jean bellowed laughter. Coiling rope and tossing it neatly into his boat, he exclaimed, "Who needs a pool? The ocean is the best pool of all." His arm swept grandly across the view. "Besides, you spent the first nine months of your life in water. Every human being on earth is born knowing how to swim. It's time for you to remember, American."

Then, as if Bryan were another piece of rope, he swiftly picked him up and pitched him into the ocean.

*Chapter
Ten*

"It's a good thing I made a reservation," Winston said.

He and Denise contemplated the cavernous dining porch. Half the wicker tables and chairs were draped with sheets. The rest were just empty.

Arnaud, the sleepy-looking man who seemed to constitute the entire staff, brought them a pot of coffee. Sort of.

Winston tasted the tepid, pale-brown liquid. "Whoever decided to call this coffee should be busted for violating the truth-in-labeling laws." He sighed dramatically. "Do you know what I would give for a cup of Isabella's cappuccino right now?"

"Oh, well," Denise said consolingly. "I guess uncoffee is the right thing to drink after a night on a nonmattress. So what do you want to do to work off this sumptuous breakfast? Go for a swim in the water-free pool or play tennis on the no-net court?"

"How much time do we have to kill?" Winston asked. "And I do mean kill."

"I think the ship is supposed to dock around ten," Denise said. Yawning, she glanced at her watch. "So we've got less than an hour if we want to be there to greet our friends. I bet Isabella's ready to call out the Coast Guard."

"And Bryan probably has his revolutionary army ready to go to war with somebody, anybody. I hope they don't fire on Izzy's Coast Guard."

Denise looked at him with amused tenderness. "Winnie, has anyone ever suggested that you have a great future writing scripts for bad movies?"

"The words have occasionally been murmured in my ear. With emphasis on the word *bad*." Eyeing a piece of toast, Winston decided nothing that soaked with margarine was meant to be eaten.

"Come on," he said, reaching for Denise's hand. "Let's go find our friend Arnaud and ask him exactly where the ship lands. It's got to be someplace deeper than where we left the dinghy."

"And we have to arrange to get the dinghy back to the man who rented it to us," Denise added.

"And pay the bill for our deluxe accommodations and unforgettable breakfast," Winston said.

144

"All in all, a thrilling morning," Denise said. "We must remember to bring the children here someday."

As lightly as Denise had said those words, and as ghastly as the setting was, Winston's heart did a somersault for joy.

How did it happen, Egbert? You really, truly are the luckiest man on earth.

Bryan stood shivering and blue lipped at the edge of the dock.

"Maybe I should try it once more," he called.

"I think you've got the hang of it," Jean protested happily. "But okay, here goes. One . . . two . . . three. Overboard!"

"Whoopee!" Bryan shouted as he hit the water. This time he didn't resist at all; he let the four-foot depth claim him as if it were his natural environment. He surfaced, sputtering and laughing, with a single thought. *If Nina could see me now!*

Paddling back to the dock, he began to ask for just one more toss into the water. But Jean cut him off.

"We've been doing this for half an hour. We must work!" he said severely. "As it is, you are probably the only big fish I will reel in today. So don't ask me to throw you back."

Bryan flopped down on the dock, suddenly exhausted. But he felt great, too. The terror he had experienced only minutes ago, when Jean had first pitched him into the water, had given way to pure delight. And he was enjoying Jean's company, too. For all the differences in their backgrounds, they had a lot to talk about.

"I can't believe I've spent the last half hour doing something that even remotely resembled swimming. And it's actually fun!"

Jean handed him a faded blue towel. "We all must confront our fears. And we all must learn how to have fun."

"You sound a lot like my girlfriend." Bryan thoughtfully rubbed the circulation back into his legs. "She keeps telling me that I won't really be liberated until I can have fun."

"Perhaps I can quote that for the essay I am writing," Jean said.

"What essay?"

"On the real meaning of liberation. It is part of my application form. I am trying to win a scholarship to the University of Miami." He sighed. "If I finish in time. Writing does not come naturally to me."

Bryan stared at Jean as his new friend efficiently went about readying his boat. "But why? What do you need college for? You already know more than any professor I ever met. You know how to live, man! There's a saying, 'If it ain't broke, don't fix it.' Why do you want to go improving a perfect life?"

"It looks perfect to you, because you're just living it for a day or two. But fishing is a hard life. If there is a red tide or something upsets the balance of nature, I am in deep trouble. I can't call in sick because I am the only one who works for my employer—me." Jean thumped his chest for emphasis. "And the wholesalers who buy what I catch—I'm at their mercy."

"I guess that's true," Bryan had to acknowledge, although he was reluctant to see the bubble burst.

"Besides, my girlfriend is already at U Miami. She is studying to be a marine biologist. She looks awfully good in a wet suit. I'm afraid of what will happen if I leave her alone up there."

Bryan's good mood all but evaporated as he thought about Nina. "I guess I'm sort of in the same position," he said. "Academically I'm equal to Nina. But she can do an awful lot that I can't do. Anything involving deep water, for instance."

"You're a good student?" Jean asked, a smile on his face.

"Too good, Nina says. She complains that I'd rather study than do sports. And that I'd rather write a manifesto than do almost anything."

"So let's make a deal!" Jean exclaimed. "Isn't that what they say on American TV?" He looked very pleased with himself. "You help me write that essay—"

147

Bryan got it. "And you teach me how to swim!" he finished.

"What ship?" the desk clerk asked Winston and Denise. An unlit cigarette dangling from his lips, the clerk-cum-waiter projected a maddening air of indifference.

"The *Homecoming Queen*," Winston repeated. "The ship that stops here today so the passengers can shop."

Arnaud snickered. "Shop? For what, palmetto bugs? I guess I could unlock the old gift shop. We're having a special sale on vintage Belgian chocolates. If the mice didn't get 'em."

"Are you trying to tell us that the *Homecoming Queen* doesn't stop here today?" Denise asked.

"Or tomorrow or the next day," Arnaud said. He shifted the cigarette to the other side of his mouth.

"But it's on the printed schedule," Winston said.

"Oh, on the printed schedule," Arnaud sneered.

Winston fought back panic and fury. "Well, then we may have to talk our way onto a different cruise ship," he stated, projecting as much authority as he could muster. "Who's scheduled to stop here next?"

"You don't seem to get it," the clerk said. "Nobody stops here."

"Winston . . ." Denise said slowly. "I'm getting a funny feeling." She turned to Arnaud. "We thought that this was Juma. But it's not, is it?"

"Give the lady a cigar," Arnaud said. "Juma's ten miles thataway." He pointed out at the infinite sea. "This here's Pleasure Island. Pleasure's our name and pleasure's our aim. We've got T-shirts that say it, if you want 'em."

Isabella sighed with relief at the sight of Jason and Nicole hand in hand. For once they looked like a pair of honeymooners-in-training.

She was also relieved to see Danny relaxing for a change. Finally the four of them had the air of mindless contentment that a Caribbean cruise was supposed to produce.

The *Homecoming Queen* was anchored at Juma, and from what Isabella had read and could see, it was going to be their best stop yet. The island was famous for snorkeling, and many different guides competed for the tourists' dollars with colorful signs.

The island also boasted a fruit, vegetable, and spice market with such exotic delights as fresh sugarcane, star fruit, a dozen varieties of mangoes, and tender young gingerroot. Up in the hills that dotted the skyline were famous ruins. A small but renowned museum offered glimpses of household artifacts dating back to antiquity.

149

The one disappointment on Juma was that there was no sign of Denise and Winston among the throng of visitors and natives in the harbor. *I'd give anything to see those hideous neon green shorts of Winston's,* Isabella realized with a pang.

She tried comforting herself with the knowledge that the ship would remain anchored at Juma until the next morning—as Denise no doubt knew perfectly well. *And if you're not back by then,* she mentally telegraphed her friend, *we're staying put until you show up. I'm not leaving Juma without you.*

Having made that vow, she joined Danny, Jason, and Nicole in a friendly debate as to which snorkeling guide sounded the most appealing.

"I vote for Cap'n Bob," Danny said, pointing to a dolphin-shaped sign with bright blue lettering. "He sounds like the real thing."

"What about that Cap'n Albert?" Jason vied. "I like his motto: We'll teach you how to snorkel even if you're a New York'l."

"You chauvinists are missing the boat," Isabella said. "My vote goes to Cap'n Rose. Look at her picture on that billboard. I bet she knows the whereabouts of every fish within a hundred miles. Don't you think, Nicole?"

Nicole shrugged. "Whatever you guys decide. Snorkeling's not really my thing. Frankly, I think the market sounds more interesting. But I want to be where my sweetie is." She leaned her head on Jason's shoulder.

"Well, let's make our pick and get going," Danny said, leading the way to the gangplank.

Where they all but collided with Tom Watts.

"Jess, are you sure you feel okay?"

"I feel fine," Jessica repeated, for what felt like the hundredth time. "I'm just not in the mood for shopping."

"You don't need something for the dance tonight?"

"You're the one who keeps complaining that I took all the hangers in the closet," Jessica pointed out to her twin. "I have a dozen dresses I can wear. Or I can wear your new pink thing."

Elizabeth didn't rise to the bait. "But the museum—" she began.

"And I'm not in the mood for sightseeing," Jessica said firmly. "Really, Liz. You go ahead with Todd. I'm going to stay here and read."

"A book?"

"No, the back of a cereal box," Jessica returned scathingly. "That's a little insulting, Liz. I have been known to read a book voluntarily. Once."

"Okay, okay," Elizabeth said, resigned. Standing in front of the mirror, she tied a bright green scarf around her hair and then took it off again. "How do I look?"

Jessica eyed her shrewdly. "Undecided."

"What does that mean?" Elizabeth asked.

"Oh, you know. As though you're not sure you really want Todd back but you want him to want you."

"Wow." Elizabeth gave her a respectful look. "What was the one book you read, the complete writings of Sigmund Freud?" Glancing at the folding alarm clock on the dresser, Elizabeth hastily threw sunglasses, sunblock, and a notepad into her new straw shoulder bag. "I'm late. Are you absolutely pos—"

"Good-bye, Liz," Jessica said firmly. "Have fun. Don't hurry back."

Elizabeth shot her one more quizzical look, then closed the door behind her.

Denise patted the dinghy on the prow. "Hi, there. Thanks for waiting."

"You're sure we're doing the right thing?" Winston stared at the horizon. "I'd feel a lot better if we could see where we were going."

"As soon as we get around to the other side of this island, we will. Are you going to help me with the sail or just stand there looking gorgeous?"

"Just stand here looking gorgeous," Winston said.

"That's probably just as well," Denise said. "I love you, Winston. We'll be fine, I promise. Juma by lunchtime, or my name is mud."

*　　*　　*

Jessica paced the cabin. *Wait*, she cautioned herself. *Wait until they've all gone ashore.*

She brushed her hair a hundred strokes, made a French braid, then unplaited it and brushed another hundred strokes. That used up sixteen minutes.

She pulled the braid apart, jumped into the shower, and washed her hair. And washed her hairbrush just to use up another couple of minutes.

After blowing her hair dry and deciding not to rebraid it, she put her ear to the door. She could still hear footsteps. "Come on, guys," she wanted to call out. "All ashore for shell jewelry and corny T-shirts."

As Jessica paced some more, her eye fell on Elizabeth's bunkside bookshelf. She idly looked through the books. It would be nice to tell the studious Wakefield that her no-brain twin had been as good as her word and actually read a book.

Unfortunately Elizabeth's traveling library contained mostly poetry—little leather-bound volumes of the old eighteenth-century stuff that she and Tom were forever reading to each other.

Opening a volume of John Dryden's work, Jessica quickly concluded that the word *dry* had probably been derived from his name. But just as she was about to toss it aside, the book fell open to a poem called "Song of Jealousy, in Love Triumphant."

The rhythm and rhyme caught her up. She realized that if the words had been set to rock music, the poem wouldn't be half bad.

> *What state of life can be so blest*
> *As love, that warms a lover's breast?*
> *But if in heaven a hell we find,*
> *'Tis all from thee,*
> *O Jealousy!*
> *'Tis all from thee,*
> *O Jealousy!*

"'Tis all from thee, O Jealousy!'" she repeated aloud. The words seemed to sum up the cruise. If not life itself.

And it wasn't just Tom and Nicole who were inspiring jealousy. Bryan had been jealous of that doctor, Richard Daniels. And Isabella was jealous of the attention Danny was paying to Jason. Most likely other little jealous scenarios were going on all around her.

She herself was admittedly jealous—of nearly everyone. Because it was too ridiculously unfair to be on a divinely romantic cruise without a boyfriend.

And that was why she had stayed behind on the

ship that morning. While her shipmates explored Juma, Jessica could explore their cabins. Slowly and thoroughly.

She wouldn't give up until she found the shirt that was missing that all-important button, snug in the right front pocket of her denim cutoffs.

The big dance, the most important social event of the cruise besides the wedding, was going to take place that night. As the music swelled under the starlit sky Jessica intended to be in Mr. Mystery's arms.

Tonight—and forever after.

"Hi!" Jason said affably, as if a glimpse of Tom were all he needed to cap a beautiful day.

Tom's mouth stretched in a painful-looking grin. "Hi!" he said. He looked at the others, then opened and closed his mouth. "Hi!"

"Hi!" Nicole said, blushing furiously.

"Hi," Danny growled.

"Hi!" Isabella sang out operatically, vainly trying to cover the growl.

As the "hi" chorus faded away, the little group stood stone silent. Feet shuffled. Cheek muscles tensed. Finally Tom took in a big gulp of air and broke the uncomfortable hush.

"Are you, um—" He looked from face to face, as if searching for words to fill out a suddenly diminished vocabulary. "Are you going to, ah, town?"

157

"We're going snorkeling," Jason declared, still oblivious to the tension that was gripping the others. "Want to join us?"

Oh, no! Isabella screamed inside her mind. *Don't do it, Tom! Danny might cut your air hose!*

"Gee, thanks, but I don't think so," Tom said. "I thought I'd head to the market."

Jason turned to Nicole. "You said you'd rather go to the market than go snorkeling, honey. Why don't you go with Tom?"

Isabella clamped her hand to her mouth.

"I want to be with you, Jason," Nicole protested.

"Don't be silly, hon. Why should you do something that bores you? I'll explore the coral reef, you'll explore the coral earrings, and we'll have lots to tell each other over dinner."

"But Jason—"

Jason gave her a little shove. Clearly he didn't notice the bright tears gathering at the corners of her eyes. "We have a lifetime to be together. Don't worry about my feelings, Nicole. I'm fine."

Your feelings, you absolute idiot! Isabella wanted to yell. *What about Nicole's feelings?*

"Please come with us, Nicole," she contented herself with saying. "Don't leave me alone with these two guys."

But it was too little, too late. As Isabella

watched in misery Nicole blinked away her tears and linked arms with Tom.

"The market sounds great," she declared, tossing her hair. "In fact, it sounds fabulous. Come on, Tom. Let's go."

After searching some twenty cabins, Jessica was tired, cranky, grossed out by male mess, and close to feeling hopeless. She'd crossed a lot of names off her list, but it seemed liked there were still hundreds more.

Spirits sinking, she formed an unpleasant thought. Maybe the only way to get another glimpse of her mystery man was to land in jeopardy again. At the very least, she was probably going to have to feign danger—maybe she *could* fall overboard again, only this time she'd wear a lifejacket under her clothes.

Discouraged but still determined, Jessica picked up her pace. She impatiently jiggled open stuck drawers and in frustration slammed closet doors shut. Who was going to hear her, anyway? Every passenger except the two in sick bay had gone ashore.

Casting a last disgusted look around cabin 84, she kicked the dresser in despair.

Then she froze in terror as the cabin door was yanked open.

*   *   *

Danny thought he might explode. As he watched Nicole strut down the gangplank with Tom, he practically vibrated with frustration. The sheer helplessness he felt was infuriating.

Jason stared at him. "Are you okay, Danny?"

"Oh, yeah, I'm fine, I'm great. Fabulous," he added, unable to resist mimicking Nicole. "My hand fell asleep, that's all. So I'm shaking it awake."

And I'd like to shake you awake, he longed to say.

Danny took Isabella into his arms, as if he were giving her a gentle hug. But the words he whispered into her ear were hardly romantic. "Are you happy now? Is this what you wanted to happen?"

"Shhh," she hissed. "Just act normal."

"Normal? You mean act stupid?"

She placed one of her sandaled feet on one of his sneakered ones. "I am going to come down on your toes with all my weight if you don't shape up right now. Jason is starting to look bewildered."

"How would you look if the love of your life were heading off to a motel with someone else? I've got to tell him the truth about her."

"Motel! They're going to hang out with fruits and spices, for pete's sake! And you promised me!"

"If you—" he began, when he felt her foot come down on his toes. "All right, all right," he

160

whispered harshly, "I'll keep my promise. But we're going to act as chaperones."

Danny turned to Jason and smiled. "I just persuaded Isabella that Nicole had the right idea. We can snorkel anywhere. But how often do you get to look a star fruit in the eye? We're all going to the market."

"Well, well," sneered the burly red-haired steward who stood there sizing Jessica up. "What have we here?"

Jessica's heart was pounding so rapidly, she could barely breathe. "You scared me!" she cried indignantly. "Next time knock, will you?"

"That's a good one," the man said, showing teeth. "Ha ha. Did you knock? Or did you let yourself in with your little key?"

"You've been spying on me." She stamped her foot. "I don't appreciate that at all."

The steward, who couldn't have been much older than she was, looked as if he were about to spit nails. "You know, you college kids disgust me," he said. He crossed his muscular arms across his chest. "All the money in the world, but that isn't enough for you. And now some shrink will tell the court that you weren't really stealing because you're a klepto."

It began to dawn on Jessica that the man wasn't fooling around. She'd been looking for trouble, and here it was. But her guardian angel wasn't on hand to rescue her.

"You think I'm a thief, is that it? Well, who could blame you?" she said, with an attempt at an ingratiating laugh. "I'm not, though, and I'll prove it." She pulled the pockets of her jeans inside out. They were empty except for the sacred button, which rolled across the floor and out of sight.

"There. Are you satisfied?" she asked. "Nothing except a button. Which you made me lose." Sudden tears sprang to her eyes.

Shifting uneasily, the steward seemed to reconsider. But apparently he wasn't ready to let her off. "If you're not a thief, what are you doing in everybody's cabin?" he asked suspiciously.

"It's none of your business," Jessica snapped, scanning the floor for the button.

"In that case, it's the captain's business."

Jessica snapped back to attention. The captain was handsome, and she wouldn't mind going to see him, but being hauled to his office by an irritated steward wasn't the best way to introduce herself.

Tilting her head at its most sincere angle, she dredged up her favorite pleading-for-mercy voice. Parents, principals, friends—everyone had heard that voice.

"I'm looking for my boyfriend," she said. "You

probably won't believe me . . ." She lowered her eyes. "But it happens to be the truth. We're playing a kind of hide-and-seek with each other, you see. He won't tell me what cabin he's in, so I'm trying to figure it out. It's a game, that's all, and I'm terribly sorry if it got you upset."

The steward looked her up and down. "It's crazy enough to be the truth," he muttered. "I'll tell you what," he went on. "Give me his name and I'll get his cabin number from the manifest. It'll cost you twenty bucks, but you'll win the game."

I don't have his name, Jessica wailed inwardly. *That's the problem!*

"Thanks," she improvised hastily. "But that would be cheating, and I never cheat. I have to find his cabin on my own."

Finally catching sight of the button, she swiftly bent to scoop it up. Then she broke past the man and ran down the narrow corridor.

It was only later that she realized how foolish she had been. The steward had been asking for twenty dollars to buy his silence.

Why did she always realize these things too late?

Chapter Twelve

Todd didn't realize that he had forgotten his camera until he and Elizabeth had already left the ship and started walking toward Juma's huge outdoor market. As they strolled down the quaint village street, Todd wished he could snap some pictures.

Without corroborating evidence, he was going to have a hard time believing that the day had truly happened. Brilliant red poincianas bloomed among the ancient stones of the town's many squares. Flamingos strutted along the snow-white beach, comical yet elegant on their spindly legs.

Nature, for all its splendor, wasn't the real showstopper, however—not for Todd.

If he had a camera, thirty-five out of thirty-six shots would have featured Elizabeth Wakefield. He wouldn't have included her in the thirty-sixth, just to show how her absence diminished a landscape.

Elizabeth had never looked more alluring. Although her outfit was unremarkable—a simple green T-shirt, khaki walking shorts, and green suede sandals—she managed to look stunning. Her California freshness was positively luminous in the clear Caribbean air.

If anything proved that beauty was more than skin deep, it was that Elizabeth was more beautiful than her identical twin. At least that was how Todd perceived her.

As they walked, Elizabeth took his hand. And it seemed like the most natural thing in the world for her to do.

"Let's go to the market," she said. "I'd like to buy some spices for Steven and Billie." Todd knew that Elizabeth's older brother and his girlfriend avidly liked to cook, the more exotic the better.

"Sure," Todd said indulgently. "Whatever you want."

"It's a nice change to hear someone say that," Elizabeth said. "I feel like the theme song for this cruise has been 'Whatever You Want, I Don't Want.'"

"I know what you mean." Todd nodded.

"And it's nice to hear those words too," Elizabeth said. "You always did know what I meant." She glanced at him. "Well, almost always," she added.

Just as Todd and Elizabeth had done through

166

years of high school, they naturally hit the same stride. Both long legged and energetic, they bounced along the curving road in perfect tempo. It was as if they were listening to the same music.

Their fingers comfortably twined around each other's. Sensing the warmth of Elizabeth's soft palm against his own, Todd felt familiar stirrings of desire.

But he couldn't help thinking of Gin-Yung for a moment, as hard as he was trying to keep her off his mind. And he couldn't help wondering whether he really wanted Elizabeth or whether wanting her was just a habit—a routine he should have outgrown.

He was relieved when they turned a corner and found themselves in the midst of the bustling market. The quiet walk had allowed him too much time to analyze the situation he'd found himself in.

Colorful spices, heaped to overflowing in the various stalls, were everywhere. Brightly dressed sellers hawked their goods, genially insulting their competitors in an effort to win business.

"Get your red-hot chili pepper here. It'll make you live to be a hundred and father twenty children."

"His ginger tastes like sawdust. If you want flavor, buy mine!"

Elizabeth studied the bins. "I can't remember

whether Billie loves cardamom and hates coriander, or loves coriander and hates cardamom."

"Why not buy her both to be on the safe side? She can always give away the one she hates."

"Good idea," Elizabeth said. "I—" Her voice suddenly faltered.

"What is it, Liz?" he asked.

"Oh, nothing," she said brightly. "I just saw Tom and Nicole over there. Where the coconut carvings are." Her voice sounded two octaves higher than usual.

Todd followed her gaze. *Nothing,* he echoed to himself with heavy irony as they both watched Nicole handing money to a vendor.

"Want to talk about it?" he asked Elizabeth.

She gave a masterful imitation of a casual shrug. "What's to talk about?" she said in that unnaturally bright voice. "Over is over. And what isn't over isn't over," she added, gazing into his eyes.

He knew she believed the message she was sending. He also knew she was wrong.

Her indifference toward Todd was as transparent as the Caribbean waters. Tom was the one she loved.

As Todd looked at her against the exotic backdrop, he suddenly saw a truth that no camera could have captured. Yes, Elizabeth was beautiful and wonderful, and he would probably always love her, but they were no longer two halves of a couple. They were two separate individuals. Their destinies could only take them further apart, not closer together.

As the awareness took shape in his mind, a deep pang rippled through his body. Watching Elizabeth turn to buy spices for Billie, he had the odd, embarrassing sensation of being on the verge of tears.

There was something so final in what he felt. A line was being drawn, thick and dark—a border that might be crossed in only one direction.

He'd spent most of freshman year separated from Elizabeth, but in a very, very different way. He'd been stung by her refusal to sleep with him and then outraged because of her role in publicizing the sports scandal that had turned his life upside down. For a short time he'd even been smugly indifferent because he'd had Lauren Hill in his bed. Finally he'd felt heartbroken and devastated by her lack of desire to patch things up between them.

All those negative feelings were gone now, and he was glad to be rid of them. But he was left in a very complicated place. It was one thing not to be in love with Elizabeth because he was furious at her; it was another not to be in love with her even though he was filled with loving warmth for her.

He hovered in a kind of agony, then the image

of Gin-Yung's animated face floated before him. This time he didn't try to push her out of his mind. The two of them were new and still tentative, but they had . . . possibility. And a lot of electricity crackling between them.

If only Elizabeth and Tom could get back together, the four of them could probably have some great times together—but maybe that was too much to hope for. Right now, it would be enough to get Elizabeth to face the truth. Tom was the man she loved, no matter how mad she was. Tom, not Todd, was the man she wanted.

Tom hadn't felt so uncomfortable since an afternoon in his childhood when he'd rolled in a poison ivy patch. He was literally itchy, a fact that Nicole couldn't help noticing.

"Are you sure you shouldn't see the ship's doctor about that?" she inquired solicitously as he scratched his shoulders, his elbows, the back of his neck. "It could be a serious allergy."

"It's probably just the sunscreen I used," he said. "I tried some fancy new brand." Lying to her made him even itchier, but what was he supposed to say? *I'm having an allergic reaction to you, Nicole.*

It wasn't her fault. Jason had all but hurled her into Tom's arms. There was nothing to do but trek around Juma, praying that the day would end without further emotional disaster.

To make things even worse, every single item they saw in the huge open-air market seemed loaded with implications. The hammock maker tried to sell them the matrimonial model. The perfume vendor was pushing mango-scented massage oil.

The silences between them grew so awkward that Tom finally had to say something or explode. "Look, I know this isn't the day you planned, but I guess we should make the best of it. Is there anything you'd especially like to see?" He started to give the whole chamber-of-commerce spiel about the birds and the flowers, the hills and the caves.

"You don't have to baby-sit me," Nicole returned irritably. "This is my day for being dumped, so you're perfectly welcome just to go off on your own if you want."

It was exactly what Tom wanted, but he couldn't bear to tell her that. She seemed almost at the breaking point.

"Jason didn't dump you," he said kindly. "I think he really meant it about not wanting you to be bored."

"But that's the whole point!" Nicole cried. "I'm never bored when I'm with him. Even if we're just sitting around doing nothing. It's enough for me to look at his eyelashes. The trouble is, the same isn't true for him."

171

"I hate to say it," Tom began, "but maybe that's just one of those gender differences that won't go away. I think we have to concede that there are a few of those."

Nicole put her hand on his arm. "Thanks for trying, Tom, but it's no use. I'm afraid he's just not in love with me. Not getting-married, forever in love." She wiped a tear from her eye. "I bet he's just trying to work up the nerve to call the whole thing off," she added with a huge, defeated sigh.

"Nicole, that's ridiculous. What's not to love about you?" Tom said lightly. His gallantry was repaid by a wild tickling sensation right where he couldn't reach it, in the middle of his back. "It's probably a classic case of prewedding jitters," he said, wriggling like a maniac. He could have asked Nicole to scratch his back, but he didn't dare.

"Jason probably figures this is the last week in his entire life he'll get to hang out with the guys," Tom went on. "It's really no cause for alarm. Don't you have your own jitters?"

The instant he put the question, he knew he was in deeper trouble. Her lips quivered, and her skin paled a little.

"I do," she moaned, "and that's part of the problem." She looked up, down, away, everywhere but at him—then zeroed in on his eyes. She had a determined look he remembered well.

"I liked our kiss the other night," she said softly.

172

"Yeah," he said, rubbing his chin. "It was great."

His tone of voice made her giggle. "Come on, Tom. Admit it felt good."

Somewhere in the background a steel band started to play. Tom knew the melody, but he couldn't remember the name of the song.

"It did feel good," he said honestly. "It made my lips tingle. It made me wonder what would've happened if you hadn't met Jason and we'd kept dating that summer after our senior year in high school."

She started to say something, but he cut her off. He had to tell her the whole truth. "The kiss made me feel bad, too, though," he said. "Even before Elizabeth saw us and Danny punched me. It made me feel disloyal. And I hated that feeling."

As the steel band swung into the chorus, Tom recognized the song. Of course. How fitting. It was "As Time Goes By," from *Casablanca*.

Nicole recognized it too. She began to sing. "A kiss is just a kiss—"

"Everyone always gets that wrong," Tom said. It was one of the many facts he'd learned from Elizabeth. "It's 'A kiss is still a kiss.'"

"Same difference," Nicole said dismissively. "Kiss me, Tom."

"Nicole—"

"I have to know," she said. "I'm so confused, I'm going nuts. I have to know whether our kiss the other night was a last one for the road. Or a sign that I'm not ready to be a bride."

"I can't," he said hoarsely.

"Sure you can. It's simple. First you put your arms around me—"

"I can't because of Elizabeth. I love her, Nicole."

"Then you'll make everything work out, and you'll have a thousand million kisses together. The way Jason and I will. Maybe." She jabbed him lightly on the arm. "Admit that she punished you enough for two kisses."

He furiously scratched his chest, close to his heart. Then he put his arms around Nicole and kissed her.

Elizabeth felt like crying as the strains of the theme song from *Casablanca* filtered through the marketplace.

She looked at Todd. "This song is one of my all-time favorites." She could hear the tears in her own voice.

Todd nodded. "Let me guess. It's one of Tom's favorites, too. Am I right?"

"Yes," Elizabeth whispered, miserable.

If this had been any other day, she would have felt like the band was playing just for her—for her and Tom. Now it was as if the romantic song was just a cruel reminder of what could have been.

Elizabeth knew Tom had to feel the same way. He just had to.

She tried with all her might to look anywhere except in Tom's direction, but her eyes had a will of their own. Peering past mangoes, coconuts, hammocks, and parrots, she focused on the man she loved.

And saw him lean down and kiss Nicole.

That's it! That's it! she screamed silently. *I hate you, Tom Watts!*

She thrust her hands into Todd's hair, pulled his head down toward hers, and did the only thing that could possibly make her feel better.

She kissed him.

Todd closed his eyes. For one sublime moment, he surrendered to the familiar sweetness of Elizabeth's lips.

But the image of Gin-Yung floated back into his mind, haunting him. He opened his eyes. Just beyond a cluster of palms stood Gin-Yung, for real.

She was staring at him. And the expression on her face wrenched Todd's heart. As he watched, Gin-Yung turned away.

He unwound himself from Elizabeth's desperate embrace. But it was too late. Gin-Yung had disappeared into the crowd.

"Are you sure you guys don't want to go snorkeling?" Jason asked for what seemed like the hundredth time.

"Positive," Danny said grimly. "There's nothing as exciting as a big open market."

"Just looks like a horizontal department store to me," Jason complained.

Danny surveyed the vivid maze of stands radiating out before them. "Which way did they go?" he hissed to Isabella.

"Got me," she answered. She was absolutely livid. Danny and his famous ethics had gone completely over the edge.

"Wouldn't it be funny if we ran into Nicole and Tom?" Jason said cheerfully.

"Hilarious," Danny responded.

"An absolute laugh riot," Isabella said.

Jason gave the two of them a questioning look. "You guys all right?"

"Nothing wrong with us that a cappuccino won't cure," Isabella declared, anxious to steer the topic of conversation away from Tom and Nicole. "There's got to be someone out here selling cappuccino. My foamed-milk detector says go this way," she declared, making a right turn past the biggest collection of straw hats she'd ever seen. "And I can't think of a likelier place to find Denise and Winston."

As they moved through the crowd she kept hoping to catch a glimpse of her friends. She couldn't imagine that they weren't in the market somewhere.

But she didn't see Denise. Or Winston. Instead, she saw Nicole and Tom. Isabella couldn't believe her eyes. They were kissing. Again.

Right in the middle of the Juma market, with thousands of people watching, Tom and Nicole were kissing.

Isabella whirled so fast, she bumped into Jason. "I smell coffee, and it's coming from behind us." She put her hands on his shoulders and turned him a hundred eighty degrees.

"This way, Danny!" she sang out—too late.

His face looked like a thundercloud. His eyes looked · ready to shoot flames, and even from where she was standing, Isabella could tell that his jaw was clenched tight.

Kiss your chin good-bye, Tom! she thought. *You're really in trouble now.*

Noah remembered reading that the hardest task any psychologist ever had was to heal himself. Those were probably among the wisest words written by anyone about anything, he decided. It was so much easier to offer someone else comfort and advice than to solve one's own problems.

He probably shouldn't have come to the marketplace. His glance kept falling on things that would be perfect to give to Alex. At the moment Noah was staring at some handmade dolls, wishing he had a reason to buy one for her. He didn't know quite why he thought she would admire the careful stitching, the whimsical expressions on the cloth faces, but he was sure she would.

She would have before Leonardo, he corrected himself. Men who descended out of the sky in helicopters had much more interesting toys to offer than dolls. Elizabeth had told him that Alex and Leonardo were having lunch at La Tortue, the most expensive restaurant on the island.

Let her eat turtle soup, a hundred dollars a bowl, he told himself. If that was what she wanted to do, she wasn't the right woman for Noah anyway. At least, he tried to tell himself that she wasn't right for him. Instead he kept thinking about Alex's gorgeous green eyes.

"Are you going to buy that doll?" a voice next to him asked. "It's very pretty. Look at those little pockets on the apron."

Noah turned to see who was talking to him. "Oh, hi, Gin-Yung." Noah didn't know Gin-Yung well, but they'd chatted a few times during the last few days. "Do you collect dolls?"

"No. I'm not really a collector. Do *you* collect dolls?" she asked.

The tartness in her voice was unmistakable. "Do I detect a loaded question?" he asked.

"I just don't understand it," she said in a rush. "Is every man and boy a trophy collector?"

"What do you mean?"

"I mean that Todd Wilkins seemed to think I was heaven on earth. But all Elizabeth Wakefield had to do was crook her finger at him, and he went running."

"Oh, no!" Noah exclaimed sympathetically. "Are you sure you're not reading something into their relationship that isn't there anymore?"

"You men are always covering up for each other." Gin-Yung ran impatient fingers through her short, glossy hair. "I saw them with my own eyes. Kissing like crazy." She gave a chagrined laugh. "I don't know why I'm telling you all this. I'm sorry, Noah."

"Don't apologize," he said, smiling. "Everyone does it. I might as well be wearing a shirt that says, 'Talk to me.' I guess that's why I'm planning to be a psychologist. If the shoe fits, and all of that."

"You mean if the T-shirt fits," Gin-Yung said, and they both laughed.

"Do you want to get something to drink with me?" Noah asked impulsively. "Maybe we could get something that came with one of those little umbrellas." He winked. "I might even unload a little on you."

Gin-Yung nodded. "Sounds like a plan."

They made their way to a small restaurant overlooking the water and ordered drinks. Gin-Yung sipped hers thoughtfully, not saying much.

Noah drained the last succulent drops of a tall, yellow drink called a Hurricane Harry. "So what would you do if some guy invited you to a restaurant where they serve genuine turtle soup, a hundred dollars a pop? Tell me honestly, now—not just what you think I want to hear."

"What I would do is suggest that he give the hundred dollars to a wildlife preservation fund," Gin-Yung answered. "And I'd tell him to take me out for a piña colada instead."

"For real?"

"Noah, just because it was what you wanted me to say doesn't mean it isn't true."

"Ouch!" Noah laughed. "Am I that transparent?"

"Yes," Gin-Yung said promptly.

"Now, that wasn't what I wanted to hear. You get into trouble being transparent."

"That depends on what there is to see," Gin-Yung said.

"Oh, yeah? And what do you see?" he asked boldly.

"I see someone who is kind and gentle and honest and good."

"A Boy Scout, in other words." Noah wrinkled his nose. "How exciting."

Gin-Yung put her hand over his, very lightly and briefly—but nonetheless a definite contact. "Maybe it is exciting," she said slowly. "Maybe one bad boy starts to look like another after a while. And it's the good ones who really are unique."

Noah sucked at his straw again to cover his sudden flurry of feeling.

"I do believe I've flustered the doctor," Gin-Yung said impishly.

"I guess I'm not used to being analyzed," Noah said.

Gin-Yung raised her eyebrows. "Don't you like being in the hot seat?"

Noah shook his head, laughing. Gin-Yung was something special. In fact, she was almost as special as Alex. *Almost.*

Chapter Thirteen

Lila resisted the impulse to put a black mantilla over her shining hair. If she ran into Leonardo, it would be nice to look as if she'd taken his words as seriously as she had.

Then she reminded herself that white was every bit as suitable for a widow. In fact, in some cultures white was the official color of mourning. Slinging an opera-length string of pearls around her neck, Lila looked critically at herself in the mirror.

But the point wasn't to put on a show for Leonardo. And the point wasn't to look beautiful, although she couldn't help noticing how stunning she was without a single touch of color on her person.

The point was to remember that she was a widow. Tisiano deserved a grieving wife, and that's what Lila planned to be, even if it killed her.

An hour later Lila had walked through much of Juma. Making her way around the tiny island, she thought of going into a church and lighting a candle. But churches hadn't played a big part in her life with Tisiano.

A shop with the simple name Ultima on its beige awning was a much more appropriate shrine. "To each her own," she said under her breath, grasping the brass handle on the heavy glass door.

The discreetly lit interior was almost empty except for a single, rather desperate-looking clerk. He wore a gray flannel suit that would have been at home on elegant, understated Bond Street in London. He gave Lila time to move in on the Waterford crystal, then he moved in on her.

"Madame has excellent taste," he murmured. "The Kenmare pattern is one of my favorites."

Lila lifted a ship's decanter, admiring the design. With its slender neck and wide, flat base, it had been crafted to withstand the rocking and rolling of an oceangoing vessel—a bit of design genius she could particularly appreciate after a few days on the *Homecoming Queen*.

She ran her fingers over the intricately cut

surface, admiring the delicate pattern. "Actually, I prefer Castletown," she said blandly.

The clerk twitched with excitement. Lila had just mentioned the most expensive pattern of crystal by the venerable Irish firm.

"Alas, there is no ship's decanter in Castletown," he said. "As Madame doubtless knows. But we do have a smashing one in Colleen. Let me get it for you. I'm sure you'll adore it." He hurried off to a back room.

Lila took advantage of solitude to pursue widowlike feelings. "Tisiano," she murmured, raising her eyes to heaven. "I wish you were here with me. Isn't this a lovely shop?"

Lila didn't expect Tisiano to answer her question, but she thought she'd feel *something*. She'd heard lots of men and women say that when a loved one died, they could still sense the person's spirit twenty-four hours a day. But Lila didn't sense anything. There wasn't even a hint of Tisiano in the quiet shop.

Lila felt let down. If there were anyplace she should be able to communicate with Tisiano, it was in a shop like Ultima, among objects so in keeping with Tisiano's taste.

She wandered the length of the counter, stopping to admire a display of brandy snifters. They were quite the most elaborate she had ever seen. Tisiano would probably have thought they were overdone. "Vulgar," she could hear him saying, with a patrician wave of his hand.

Bruce, however, would flip for the glasses. Lila could easily imagine his delight if he opened a gift box and found one of the snifters nestled in purple velvet. Better yet, a pair—his and hers.

The clerk came back, beaming. He was a carrying a large crystal decanter. "Here—" he began.

But the thought of clinking glasses with Bruce had depressed Lila. She was only eighteen years old, and it seemed that she might never be happy again. Barely holding back her tears, she fled the shop and its unlikely pair of ghosts—Tisiano and Bruce.

Nina was on the verge of tears. "Please try that number again," she said to the switchboard operator. "You're sure you've got it right?"

"I'm sorry," he said. "It's ringing, but nobody's picking up. Is there an answering machine?"

"He hates them," Nina said bleakly. "He thinks they're yuppie." She stared helplessly at the sophisticated communications setup. She'd never seen so many wires, dials, switches, and buttons in one place. But what good did they do if they couldn't connect her with Bryan?

He should be back in Sweet Valley, but she'd tried every hour on the hour since eight o'clock in the morning. If he wasn't there, where was he? And didn't he know she'd be worried?

"I know, I'm being a pest," she said to the operator. "But could you please try once more?"

He tried. And once again there was no answer. Bryan seemed to have vanished off the face of the earth.

Nina went back to her cabin and threw herself down on her bed.

After a frenzied hour of shopping, Lila concluded that the island of Juma was conspiring against her. She'd exhausted two books of traveler's checks, but she still felt empty.

Each shop seemed to make her feel worse than the last. One store, selling beautiful silk Venetian ties, had made her feel especially guilty. The most attractive tie she saw was patterned with tiny two-seater airplanes. The design reminded her of Bruce and his Cessna, not Tisiano.

The lily-suffused perfume she bought had been introduced to her by Tisiano, but she couldn't help imagining Bruce going wild when he smelled it on the back of her neck.

And there was only one person she knew, besides herself, who would actually consider wearing a diver's wristwatch with a face carved from coral and tiny black pearls where the numbers should be. The watch was completely decadent, but it was also magnificent. And absurdly expensive.

She bought the woman's version, with a slender strap. Five minutes after leaving the shop, she went back and bought the man's version too. *For my father,* she told herself.

Bruce walked from shop to shop, spending money. He could just imagine Bryan Nelson's reaction to these elaborate expenditures. "Do you know how many islanders you could be feeding for the price of that blazer? You already have three summer-weight blazers in your closet. Are you trying to set a record?"

But Bruce wasn't Bryan, and he paid for the blazer without a qualm. He regarded his purchase as his personal contribution to the salary of the man who sold him the jacket.

But why, Bruce wondered, was he on his own, with only Bryan's unbidden voice for company? The other buyers and browsers were couples—attractive tanned twosomes like him and Lila.

She should be there with him, flattering him about the way the blazer fit, urging him further down the path of unabashed decadence. "You're buying only one?" she would say. "Look at what it does for your shoulders. Get it in green too. Get one in every color."

Bruce knew Lila should be with him—and he was certain she knew it too. It was unbelievable that she wasn't there.

Maybe all was fair in love and war, but it was pretty galling to be rejected in favor of a dead man. She'd told Bruce she just needed time, but it was hard to give her another minute. Life was short.

Bruce knew he would never be a philosopher, but the plane crash had made him see some truths. He knew now that fate was quirky. And as corny as it sounded, he believed that each second was infinitely precious.

Preoccupied, Bruce barely noticed that he had left behind the cluster of boutiques and wandered onto a street lined with galleries. He was about to turn back when he changed his mind.

There were several notable art collectors among the Patmans. Someday, in fact, he would inherit the largest privately owned trove of Josef Albers's works, among other modern masters. He liked the bold squares for which Albers was famous, but it would be nice to put his own stamp on the collection.

The gallery in front of him had a name that intrigued him immediately: Clara McIntee's

Oddities and Curiosities. The works on display inside lived up to the description. The small gallery was filled with unabashedly experimental sculptures using found objects, from seashells to torn envelopes to someone's dentures. There was even a chicken made entirely from bits and pieces of egg cartons.

The pieces were oddly beautiful. Bruce was especially drawn to a mosaiclike fish made of beach glass, its colors muted and worn smooth by time but still rich and infinitely varied.

Standing alone on a black pedestal, the sculpture was small enough to fit in Bruce's hand but powerful enough to mesmerize him. It seemed to suck in all the available light and give back more than it took.

He remembered excitedly that Albers had created collages out of broken glass, retrieved from a town dump in Germany when he was too broke to buy proper art supplies. Bruce's parents would probably be knocked out that he'd made the connection.

He approached the proprietor of the gallery, an elegant woman with cocoa-colored skin and gold-streaked hair. She sat watching him with an amused smile on her face.

"I want to buy the glass fish," he said without preamble. "How much is it?"

The woman shook her head. "I'm afraid you can't buy it, young sir."

Bruce hated being mistaken for just another college student eking out an allowance. He flashed a fat wad of bills. "I think I can."

"Oh, my," the woman said with a laugh, "you're the second one today. You Americans. You think it's always a question of money."

"What do I have to do, pass a test?" He wasn't in the mood for a sociological lecture. He just wanted to buy the fish. The woman shrugged expressively.

"Sorry," he said stiffly, putting away his money. "I thought you were here to sell."

The woman's smile got even broader. "The artist, my niece, wants to save that particular piece for a museum show. But it happens that I already have a call in to her to see if she'll change her mind."

Bruce brightened. "Hey, thanks. That's great. And I'm sorry about being rude before. It's just that I really love that sculpture." He walked around it, taking it in from every angle. He even loved the title—*Shattered Oceans*. It pretty much described how he felt without Lila. "Your niece is a talented woman."

"It's nice to have her appreciated," Clara McIntee replied. "But I have to tell you, even if she agrees to sell, the piece may not be available. Someone else has put a hold on it."

"You're kidding," he said.

"Only fifteen minutes ago, if you can imagine. A lovely young woman came in, and she was just as taken with the fish as you are. I told her to come back at noon. Now, perhaps when she hears my niece's price—if indeed Chéri agrees to sell—she'll change her mind. Or she might forget to come back. People do get dreamy on the islands."

"Well, I won't forget," Bruce said. "I'll be here at noon sharp."

He set the alarm on his watch, but he wouldn't need the reminder. He couldn't recall the last time that a single object had been so important.

And he wanted to meet the young woman who shared his passion for it. A like-minded taste in art might lead to something more.

Who could say? She might even have the power to take his mind off Lila.

"One . . . two . . . three . . . overboard!" Bryan yelled. He threw himself into the water.

As he hovered in the air for a giddy instant, then plunged downward into the sea, he felt like a child—the child he perhaps never had been. He felt free because he was safe, and safe because he was free. Somewhere between the fiftieth and the hundredth leap, Bryan yelled the notion out to Jean, for inclusion in his essay.

The fine points of swimming had come a little

more slowly, but he was definitely learning. Once Jean taught him how to float, Bryan found the trust in the water that made all the difference. He'd actually found the confidence to master breathing and blowing, and the different basic strokes.

"I think the sidestroke's your strongest," Jean commented. "Why don't you try swimming away from the dock?"

"You mean out toward the open sea?"

"Sure, why not?"

"Because it's still scary, that's why not," Bryan returned. "It's one thing to jump into four feet of water and then swim to shore." Bryan scanned the horizon. "It's another to go out there."

Jean laughed. "You don't have to go all the way to Florida. Just remember, if you feel that you're in trouble, flip over and float on your back. You can float for hours if you have to."

"Promise you'll come save me if I lose it?"

"I promise," Jean said. "How else am I going to finish my essay?"

As morning turned into afternoon Bryan conquered another hurdle. Not only did he swim out into measureless depths, he agreed to get into Jean's boat.

At first, the absence of terror was pleasure enough. Then he actually started to enjoy the boat's rhythmic motion.

And through it all ran a repeated refrain. *If Nina could see me now.*

He wished it even more when he landed the biggest catch of the day.

"Magnifique," Jean said approvingly. "My American friend is proving his worth. We have caught enough fish for the day; now we can head back to shore."

Bryan smiled as he added the large fish to the pile in the bow. He felt he was proving his worth in more ways than one—to himself.

"We are trailing seaweed," Jean called as he guided the boat toward the dock. "Unhook it, will you?"

Even with his newfound confidence, Bryan didn't love the idea of leaning over toward the water. "Why? What harm is it doing?"

"It's undignified," Jean called back. "If you fall in, you will float, just remember."

As he unhooked the seaweed Bryan was reminded of something else trailing behind a boat—skis.

An outrageous plan forming in his mind, he grinned at Jean. "Jean, I don't suppose you happen to know someone who has a ski boat?"

Jean burst out laughing. "They say there's no one more zealous than a new convert. I guess you've got religion for the water."

"Yes, I worship Neptune now. And I want to show my devotion by going out on water skis."

"They go pretty fast."

"So the worst that happens is, I fall. And if I fall"—he shifted into a perfect imitation of Jean's voice—"you will float, remember?"

Jean clapped him on the back. "Yes! And I have a friend who can set you up with everything you need."

Chapter
Fourteen

"Lila!"

"Bruce!"

"What are you doing here?"

"No, what are you doing here?"

"The fish!" they chorused.

"It's you?" Bruce said. "You're the quote, lovely young woman, unquote, who put a hold on my sculpture?"

"Your sculpture!" Lila said indignantly, yanking off her sunglasses to glare at him. "It's my sculpture!"

"Oh, yeah? What makes it yours?"

"Simple," she said. "I saw it first."

Bruce stared at her. "If you can use time as a weapon, I can use money. I should get a chance to top any price you'll pay."

"Who says?" Lila asked indignantly.

"I do."

"Well, so much for your Waterford snifters," Lila said.

His eyes widened appreciatively. "What Waterford snifters?"

"The ones you'd absolutely love. I'll tell you how to find them if I get to buy the sculpture."

Bruce folded his arms across his chest and leaned against the doorway to the gallery. "What's the big deal about some glass fish, anyway?"

"It reminds me of Venice," Lila said softly. "Tisiano knew an old man who made sculptures from bits of glass discarded on Murano." To her surprise, mentioning Tisiano's name didn't make her feel any sadness. Her attention was completely fixed on Bruce. "What about you? What made you want it?"

"I don't know. I just liked the way it caught the light. It seems magical to me." He reached out and ran a finger softly down her cheek. "And when I was told I couldn't have it, I wanted it even more."

Lila lowered her gaze. "Bruce," she said softly. "I—"

The gallery owner came to the door and looked at the two of them. She didn't seem the least bit surprised that they knew each other. "Are you going to stand out there all day, or is either of you still interested in buying the fish?" she asked.

They looked at each other. "I am," they chorused.

"The piece costs five hundred dollars, and that's my final price. If you want to haggle, go to the street market."

"Haggle!" Bruce said. "I don't think it's enough."

"I agree," Lila said. "Your niece is shortchanging herself."

"If she wanted to dress like the two of you, the price wouldn't be high enough," the woman said. Her face radiated fondness. "But all she cares about in the world is making her art."

Bruce swallowed. "You take it, Lila. You need it more."

"What I need—" she began. "What I need, no work of art can give me," she said with a sigh. "You take it, Bruce. You deserve to come away from this trip with something you want."

"You," he said.

"You," she said.

"Please."

"Really."

Shrugging, Bruce surrendered. He peeled five bills from his roll. He handed the gallery owner his money and took the sculpture from her.

He looked at the fish for a moment. Then he handed it to Lila. "Here. It's yours."

* * *

Leonardo beamed as Alex's fork collided with his. After a delicious lunch, they were sharing dessert, an airy mango soufflé with a swirl of white chocolate sauce and a sprinkle of coconut.

"*En garde,* Alessandra," he said playfully, holding his fork as if it were a sword.

The part of Alex that had once been Enid Rollins knew she ought to be on guard. Leonardo di Mondicci was smooth—too smooth. Her mother would probably call him an "operator."

But this was no time to think of her mother or anything else that could bring her down. If Leonardo was an operator—well, maybe the world needed more operators. After all, if everyone were as unoperational as Noah Pearson, the earth would come to a standstill.

Summoning the waiter with the merest flicker of an eye, Leonardo ordered one espresso and one hot water.

"You drink hot water?" she asked, surprised.

"Oh, no. You do."

"I do?"

He smiled broadly. "All the models do, you know. Because coffee and tea stain the teeth."

Alex would have loved a cup of coffee, but even without the jolt of caffeine, her heart started beating faster. "You mean, you think I might be model material?"

"Think?" he exclaimed. He flung his arms

open in a gesture of astonishment. "Think? I am amazed you are not under contract to an agency already."

"Leonardo, you must be joking."

"Obviously, your unusual beauty is not appreciated in America, *non e vero*? Just as there are Italians who typify Italy to the American market, but at home they're just another beauty."

She almost understood what he meant—enough to know she liked the message. But she wanted him to spell it out. "What are you saying, Leonardo?"

"I think you know *exactement* what. I would like to sign you for my agency in Milan. I believe you would make a wonderful model, and we are your natural market."

She had dreamed of hearing words like that. In fact, the whole day had the makings of a fantasy come true. The tropical paradise; the exclusive restaurant high on a hill, behind ancient stone walls. And, above all else, a charming man who was clearly taken with her.

Not just taken. He was actually discovering her, the way producers discovered actresses and, well, modeling agency owners discovered models.

Her metamorphosis from Enid to Alex was real. Leonardo's interest was the proof that she had completely shed her Enid cocoon. She would be Alex forever.

Better yet, Alessandra.

Even though the smell of Leonardo's rich espresso was tempting, her bland hot water was spiced by his words.

"This is my specialty," he was saying. "Finding the faces of the globe that will speak to my country. The readers of Italian *Vogue*, they will look at you and see California. You will sell a billion dollars' worth of denim."

"Only denim?" She couldn't help being disappointed. "I do so love the Italian designers."

He laughed. "And the Italians, *sì*. I can envision you perfectly in the colors of Missoni."

"Missoni," she breathed. "I used to have a Missoni sweater."

"You shall have a dozen of their sweaters. And those long flowing skirts. In all the outrageous colors."

She could see the colors perfectly—the teals and the oranges and the seaweed greens. She could feel the studio lights as the colors swirled around her. They would be hot lights shining just for her.

"What do you say to a sip of Sambucco? Or a little amaretto?" Leonardo asked. "We must toast your dazzling future."

"Um, thanks, but I don't think so," she said quickly. "You know how alcohol ages the skin." She held her breath, waiting for his reaction.

202

He nodded. "As wise as she is lovely," he said approvingly. "Then I will lift my glass to you."

Alex let out a sigh of relief. She hadn't told him about her problems with drinking, and she didn't want to tell him now.

Actually, she hadn't told him much at all. He was much more interested in talking about himself than he was in finding out about her.

But maybe that was just as well. Because the last man in her life, the one who'd glimpsed her naked soul, seemed to find her as fascinating as a trip to the dentist's office.

But this was no time to think about Noah.

She was going to be a model!

Lila hadn't cried the last time she'd mentioned Tisiano's name, but Bruce's generous gesture made her burst into tears.

Bruce stood in front of her, helpless. "That wasn't the intended effect."

"I know, I know," she said, wiping her eyes with her sleeve. "It's not your fault, Bruce. But how can I accept this from you?"

"By saying thank you. That's the custom where I come from, anyway."

She gave him a weak smile. "Thank you, Bruce. Thank you very much. But I just can't." She held out the fish.

"Really, you can, Lila. It's not a big deal. I mean, the money's nothing."

"I know that. But after what I said—about it reminding me of Tisiano. It's just not right."

Ignoring the fish, Bruce put gentle hands on her shoulders. "I would rather give you a ring, to tell you the truth. But you're obviously not ready. So I'll give you what you're willing to take."

"Bruce Patman, are you proposing to me?" Lila gaped at him. Her sniffles gave way to a fresh round of sobs.

His mouth was suddenly dry. He hadn't meant to propose—the words had just slipped out.

"Let me put it this way," he said. "Having almost died with you, I figured out that I'd much rather live with you. And forever seems the right length of time. So I guess maybe I'm proposing to propose to you. In a year. Or two . . . Meanwhile, if you would accept this fish as the traditional Patman symbol of affection—"

"Bruce, I've never loved anyone more than I love you this minute, but I can't." Her voice broke. "I just can't."

She thrust the fish into his hands and fled.

"All the comforts of home," Winston said dreamily as the *Jeanne d'Arc* put-putted along. "Wind, sun, and thou."

Denise hoped she didn't look as concerned

as she felt. She knew they'd had far too much sun today—Winston's face had turned a bright pink. And there hadn't been nearly enough wind.

The sun had started inching toward the horizon, which was definitely a mixed blessing. They wouldn't suffer any more sunburn, but in a few more hours it would be completely dark.

She craned her head, aching for the sight of land.

"What about over there?" Winston pointed. "It looks a little darker. Isn't that land?"

"Might be," Denise said. "Or it might be a wind line."

"I love the things you know, Denise. The phrase 'wind line' is so poetic."

"Right now," Denise said, "I would happily settle for some prosaic old dirt. I—uh-oh."

Winston sat up. "Uh-oh, what? Sharks?"

"Shh. Listen to the engine."

"Sounds like music to me. The Tchaikovsky violin concerto, actually."

"Well, I'm afraid the orchestra is about to pack up and go home," Denise said.

"You mean—?"

"I mean," she said as the engine sputtered and died.

Kneeling in the stern, she pulled the start chain. Nothing happened.

"We're out of gas, Winnie," she said. "That's it for the little engine that could."

"So let's hoist the sail again," Winston said.

"Only if you want to spend another night in No Pleasure Palace. The waves are taking us the right way, but the wind is blowing the wrong way."

"So—"

"So we paddle," Denise said.

Winston looked at the single weathered paddle lying on the bottom of the boat. "Blister time," he said gloomily.

"I will kiss each of your blisters," Denise said.

"I was thinking that you would do the blistering, and I would do the kiss-tering," Winston said. "Only kidding," he added hastily as she shot him a look. "I love to paddle. I might even switch to paddling as my major."

"We'll take turns," Denise said pointedly.

"So how do you want to decide who goes first? Odds-evens? Or eeny meeny miney mo?"

Denise fought back a surge of panic. She didn't want Winston to know how much trouble they were in. They couldn't have made it back to Pleasure Palace before nightfall even if they'd wanted to. And Denise didn't think she saw any land up ahead.

But it didn't make sense to pretend they had time to joke around. They had to get very serious—both of them.

206

"Winston," she said firmly, "I don't want to spoil your mood, but those streaks of red in the sky frequently signal an imminent sunset. We don't have a minute to waste."

She picked up the paddle and stuck it in the water, whistling to cover her terror.

Chapter Fifteen

Jessica had a brilliant idea. She would go to the captain and demand her money back—actually, Elizabeth's money. Because the week on the SS *Homecoming Queen* was supposed to be a romantic cruise. It said so right in the brochure. "Fine dining, duty-free shopping bargains, breathtaking tropical vistas," she read aloud. "And our floating hotel offers the classical touches of romance: moonlight, music, and mood."

She smacked the brochure against her bed—a single, boring bed with a semi-lumpy mattress. "Not just romance but 'classical' romance," she repeated.

Her whole situation was horribly unfair. If anyone on the ship was destined for romance, it should have been Jessica Wakefield. She was beautiful, talented, fun, and sexy. She was also sitting alone in a claustrophobic cabin, while everyone else in her crowd played *Loveboat*.

It was true that some of the couples weren't getting along incredibly well. In fact, most of the couples weren't. But at the moment, Jessica would have been thankful just to have someone not to get along *with*.

What she really couldn't believe was that the man of her dreams was actually on the boat. What a waste! This guy was emotional Styrofoam in the landfill of life. The two of them could be making that romantic hype come true—if he weren't putting all his energy into being invisible.

"What are you waiting for?" she wanted to shout. *I need you, I want you, I love you!* He had rescued her from the water; now he should save her from drowning in boredom. *Help!*

She heard footsteps outside her cabin and the hair on the back of her neck stood up.

Had a miracle happened? Had he heard her thoughts and come running?

Kneeling on her berth, she pulled the shutters back from the tiny porthole. The little window offered a view of the water and, more to the point, the deck. She peered hopefully and saw . . . a tall, thin man. . . .

Leonardo di Mondicci. Walking arm in arm with Alex, Leonardo almost looked like another college kid. Almost.

"Oh, no," Jessica groaned. They were all coming back from Juma. Couples headed up the gangplank two by two, just like the animals on Noah's ark.

Where is Noah, anyway? Why wasn't he with Alex?

A minute later she saw Noah walk by with Gin-Yung Suh. They were talking and laughing like old friends.

Nose pressed to the porthole window, Jessica gaped at the weird parade. Isabella and Danny were together, but so grimly entwined, they looked like a jailer and her prisoner. Nicole and Tom were walking side by side, but so far apart that a truck could have passed between them.

Jason walked alone, an unreadable expression on his face. Behind Jason was Lila. She was loaded down with packages, but even from the cabin, Jessica could tell her friend wasn't happy. Several yards behind Lila was Bruce. And he looked as though he'd just lost his best friend. Finally, Jessica saw Elizabeth and Todd boarding the ship. They were walking silently, their heads bent.

Jessica turned away from the porthole and picked up the brochure again. Maybe they should all ask for their money back—Elizabeth's money, that was.

The thought offered a small amount of comfort. At least she could go to the dance that night and not feel like the only one on the sidelines.

Maybe the fact that everyone else's love lives had taken a turn for the worse meant that hers would finally take a turn for the better. If that was the case, she planned to be prepared.

Jessica walked to the closet, humming. She had to figure out what she was going to wear.

"I don't believe you!" Danny yelled at Isabella. "You're still trying to muzzle me?"

Isabella struggled to stay calm. One of them had to be rational, and it looked as though she'd been elected. "I'm still trying to keep you from making an enormous mistake," she said. "Don't you get it?"

"I'm not the one who's making a mistake! Jason is! And I won't let him do it. I've got to tell him what Nicole really is!"

"And I suppose you think he'll thank you. You're crazy!" Isabella cried. "You know all those Greek plays in which the messenger gets killed because he brings bad news? That's what's going to happen to you. It'll be the end of your friendship, for sure. Not to mention what happens to you and me."

"Izzy—" Danny began explosively, then clamped his mouth shut. Shaking his head, he just looked at her. "Isabella," he said in a strangled voice, "I seriously don't get it. You can no longer claim it was one little kiss. They—"

"One, two, who's counting?" she interjected, with a lightness she didn't feel.

Danny didn't smile. "It's not funny, Isabella. It really isn't. It was like a conscious effort to humiliate Jason. I mean, Tom and Nicole couldn't have picked a more public place to kiss. What's next, a billboard? Or maybe an announcement over the loudspeaker? 'Now hear this. Now hear this. At twenty-two-hundred hours, Tom and Nicole will kiss in the grand ballroom.'"

"I know it looks bad, Danny—"

"Looks bad? Looks bad? It is bad!" He stopped and stared into her eyes. "But maybe you don't think so," he said slowly. "Maybe the woman I love doesn't feel the same way I do about fidelity. Maybe you and Nicole are sisters under the skin."

Isabella's eyes widened. "Take it back," she whispered. "Right now."

Danny shook his head. "I'm sorry, I didn't mean—I do take it back. I love you."

He put his arms around her. His lips approached her mouth.

Kiss me, Danny, she thought. *Kiss me and make it all right.*

A knock sounded at the door.

*　　*　　*

Jason looked as if he were about to explode. "Danny, I've got to talk to you. Alone," he added, with an apologetic look at Isabella.

"Sure," she said easily. "Over to you." Then, under the cover of a good-bye kiss, she pinched Danny's arm. "Silence unto death," she hissed dramatically before closing the door behind her.

"I don't get it with these women," Jason burst out. "What's on her mind? You guys aren't having trouble, are you?"

"Oh, absolutely not. It's just a line from a play she was in once," Danny said, flustered. "Don't worry about us."

"Well, I wish I could say the same." Jason groaned. "I'm really worried, man. I think Nicole's getting cold feet. She's acting so bizarre. I thought the cruise would be the final thing to pull us together, but it seems to be doing just the opposite. Now I'm terrified she's going to call off the wedding."

Danny felt like shouting for joy. But it would have taken a very hardhearted person not to feel sympathy for Jason. He looked totally stricken.

"Gee," Danny said. "I'm sorry."

"Sorry?" Jason flung the word back in his face. "We don't have time to be sorry. We've got to do something."

"Do something?" Danny echoed inanely.

"Listen," Jason said. "You know what they say about cold feet, don't you?"

Danny shook his head, worried.

"The longer you stand around, the colder you get. We've got to get Nicole moving, Danny—right down the aisle." He grabbed Danny by the elbow and shook him. "Once she's legally mine, those feet will warm right up!"

Oh, you bet they will, Danny was dying to say. *She'll hot-foot it over to Tom's.*

Jason tightened his grip on Danny. "So clearly there's only one thing to do," he said, his words coming faster and faster. "You and I are going to find the captain."

When Danny just stood there, Jason shook him again. "Come on, dude, grab the ring. I'm getting married tonight!"

When Nina heard the knock on her cabin door, she jumped up. *Please let it be Bryan. Or at least a message from Bryan saying he's safe.*

Opening the door, she felt the spirit drain out of her. A steward was holding out a white rectangular box with a cellophane lid. She could smell the heavy scent of gardenias even before she glimpsed the waxy white petals of the flowers.

And she could read the card even before she opened it. It would say some sentiment like, "Save

215

the waltz for me." The card would be signed, "Love, Richard."

She couldn't accept the expensive flowers. Especially since she had no intention of going to the dance.

She pulled two dollars out of her purse and gave it to the steward. "Sorry you made the trip for nothing, but these flowers aren't for me."

Not the real me, she added to herself. She sighed, realizing she would do anything to read just one of Bryan's long, passionate manifestos.

An eternity seemed to pass before Danny found his voice.

"The ring," he said. "The ring!" he said again, as a lightbulb went off in his mind.

Inspiration had struck.

"The ring," he said a third time, infusing his voice with sorrow. He bit his lip and stared at the floor. "Jason," he said, "I hardly know how to tell you, but the ring—well, the ring is gone."

Jason gaped. "The ring? Gone?"

"I feel so terrible," Danny moaned. "I couldn't feel worse if it had belonged to my own grandmother."

"Great-grandmother," Jason corrected. "But what happened to it?"

"It was in my drawer before I left for Juma, but when I got back, it was gone." Danny squeezed his eyelids hard enough to produce an actual tear. "It's all my fault," he said, conspicuously wiping away the moisture. "I never should have left the ship."

"Well, everyone left the ship," Jason said, in a voice that was clearly meant to make Danny feel better and therefore made him feel even worse.

"It was okay for the others to leave," Danny said. "But I should have stayed. I had a sacred duty—to guard that ring. I can't tell you how sorry I am."

Jason feebly patted him on the back. "Don't have a nervous breakdown about it," he said. Then he frowned. "Oh, wow. My parents are going to be bummed."

Danny didn't want to think about parents. Certainly not about his own, who had brought him up to tell the truth.

"You're sure it's gone?" Jason said. "You didn't move it to another drawer and then forget?"

"It had its own special spot," Danny said. *Where it's still safe and sound,* he added mentally. "I know I didn't move it. Isabella didn't move it. Much as I hate to pass the blame, I'm afraid it must have been stolen."

"I'm sure you're right," Jason said. "But why don't I check again with you? The box is so small, it could have gotten lost inside a sock." He started toward the bureau.

Danny blocked his way. "Jase, if you don't mind, there are, ah, things of Isabella's—" He blushed and cleared his throat. "Believe me, we looked through those drawers, top to bottom. Even pulled them out and looked behind them."

It was amazing how his lie had taken on a life of its own. He could visualize himself making the search as if it really had happened. "I looked through them," he repeated. "And Isabella went through them, and—sorry as I am to say it—the ring is definitely gone."

"Well, don't beat yourself up about it," Jason said. "I guess someone overheard me blabbing about it. Then when the ship was empty, they broke into your cabin."

A fresh look of concern crossed his face. "I just hope whoever it was didn't hock it in Juma. We'd better go report it to the captain. Come on!"

Chapter Sixteen

Jessica loved dances. And her favorite moment was when she walked into the room and felt a ripple go around it. Tonight was no exception. As she strolled into the ballroom, she could feel every eye in the room on her. Her short black dress showed off every curve in her body, and the straps of her silver evening sandals wound delicately around her ankles.

As she glanced around the ballroom, Jessica had to admit that for once the SS *Homecoming Queen* was living up to its hype. The ballroom looked romantic. It looked classically romantic.

The huge space had been transformed into a movie set right out of the Fred Astaire and Ginger Rogers era. The ceiling, covered with twinkling lights, rivaled the Caribbean sky. Papier-mâché palm trees were festooned with enormous paper blossoms. And the walls had been artfully draped with fishing nets. Models of starfish, mermaids, and dolphins leapt from the folds.

A live band played on a small stage at the edge of the already packed dance floor. Jessica closed her eyes, savoring the beauty of the night.

She held her pose just inside the ballroom's double doorway long enough to make sure that she'd registered on every male in the room, and then she headed toward the bar. Once she had a glass of champagne, she would start to circulate. She wasn't all that crazy about the taste of champagne, but she loved the way the sparkling gold liquid looked in her hand.

She silently vowed to dance to every song. She was going to try to forget about her frustrating search for her guardian angel and enjoy herself. If her mystery man wanted to come forward, she wouldn't be hard to find.

"Hey, Jess." Isabella's voice broke through Jessica's thoughts.

"Hi, Izzy. What's up?"

"Nothing. Everything. Who knows anymore?" She shrugged.

"What exactly happened on Juma today, anyhow? Everyone came back looking like zombies."

"Didn't you talk to Liz after she got back?"

Jessica shook her head. "No, she never came back to the cabin."

"Tom and Nicole kissed again at the market today. I think the whole ship saw them," Isabella said, her voice grim.

"Jeez! Could things get any worse?" Jessica asked. She struggled to hold on to her good mood.

"They'll probably get worse before they get better," Isabella answered. "I'll see you later."

"Yeah, see you later," Jessica said to Isabella's receding back.

I will be happy. I will be happy, Jessica said to herself. All she needed was a dance partner and she could push everyone else's worries out of her mind.

When Captain Luke Avedon approached her, she was distinctly relieved. The captain was extremely attractive, and he wouldn't have any bad news about her friends.

Besides, it made sense that the most important person on the ship should ask her to dance—and she hoped her mystery man was there to witness her moment of glory.

But the captain didn't take her into his arms. He didn't even smile at her.

"Ms. Jessica Wakefield?" he asked, in a voice that was strangely foreboding. The music stopped—or was that just her imagination? Suddenly she felt like the center of attention, but not at all in the way she had imagined.

"That's me," she said, with a perkiness she didn't feel. The captain's cold stare was making her feel like a rapidly deflating balloon.

"Come with me," Captain Avedon said.

The music started up again, and the people around her turned back to their partners.

Suddenly she very much wanted to see Elizabeth. Unfortunately, her twin was nowhere in sight.

"I don't want to make a scene, Ms. Wakefield," the captain said. "I must insist that you come with me. Now."

He already had made a scene, but she had a feeling it would be smarter not to tell him that. Jessica straightened her shoulders, threw back her head, and followed him out of the ballroom.

Moments later they entered the captain's large and elegant office. Jessica's heart sank when she saw the red-haired steward leaning against a large mahogany desk. *Why didn't I just give that guy twenty dollars?* she asked herself.

"Look, I can explain everything—" she began.

Captain Avedon raised his eyebrows. "Everything? I thought it was only a matter of a ring." He looked at the ship's purser, a tall, fair-haired man with chiseled features that Jessica would have found attractive if he weren't looking at her with total contempt.

"The ring is the only loss that's been reported,

sir," the purser said. "But that doesn't mean there aren't others. According to Federico, this young woman visited three dozen different staterooms today."

Forty-six, actually, Jessica mentally corrected.

Sitting behind his immaculate desk, the captain folded his hands and looked sternly at Jessica. "I had hoped to avoid a scandal by asking you to give back the ring. But if there are other thefts—" He shook his head. "The passengers will want more than restitution. I might have to have you arrested."

"Arrested!"

"A process with which you are no doubt familiar," the purser said coldly.

Jessica's heart pounded. She had no idea what ring he was talking about. But she had a terrible feeling she was about to find out.

"You're awfully quiet," the captain said. "Did you pocket so many rings, you don't know which one I'm talking about?"

"Of course not," Jessica protested. "I haven't taken any rings."

This time it was the purser who pounced. "What did you take, then? Watches? Cash?"

Jessica reeled. She'd been in nightmare situations before, but this one ranked with the worst of them. On top of everything else, she could hear the strains of the band and the sound of rippling laughter. How come she was in here getting the third degree while everyone else was having fun?

"I don't know why you're treating me this way," she said indignantly. "But I know that you can't get away with it. I have rights. My brother Steven is prelaw," she added sternly.

"Lady, that's a good thing," the purser said. "Because your type needs a lawyer in the family."

The captain waved him quiet. "Let me handle this, Nelson." He looked at Jessica. "Perhaps it's not too late to avoid arrest. The young man whose ring was stolen is more interested in having it back than in pursuing justice. A wedding is hanging in the balance."

"Oh, my gosh." Jessica put her hand to her mouth. "You mean Jason's ring?"

The three men exchanged smirks.

"Exactly," Captain Avedon said. "If you will be good enough to produce it, along with everything else you have taken, and if you promise that under no circumstances will you enter anyone's cabin but your own, then we may be able to close the matter."

"Sir, with all due respect," the purser said, "I don't think her promise would be worth the paper it would be written on."

"Oh, I get it," Jessica said, looking from the captain to the purser. "One of you tries to soften me up by being nice, and the other tries to scare me. And you," she cried, pointing to the steward, "tried to blackmail me for a lousy twenty bucks." She flung her arms across her chest. "This is not my idea of 'classically romantic,' I can tell you that!"

The captain smiled briefly. "Ms. Wakefield. Why don't you just turn over the ring and let us get on with the business of pleasure?"

"How can I give you what I don't have?" she asked.

"I suspected as much," the purser said, with undisguised satisfaction. "She hocked it on Juma. Quite the old hand at this sort of thing, are you?"

"Captain Avedon," she said through her teeth, "I don't have the ring because I never took it. The only thing I took on this ship that didn't belong to me was my sister's pink strapless dress. And she made me give it back."

The steward jumped up and down. "Then why was she in all the men's cabins? Looking for other dresses?"

"If you must know, I was looking for a shirt," Jessica said icily.

The purser's lips curved in a supercilious smile. "A shirt. You were looking for a shirt. You—collect shirts?"

"No!" Jessica shouted impatiently. "I only wanted one shirt. To go with my button. Don't you understand? The mystery man's shirt. The one who saved me from drowning!"

"Ah, yes," the purser said. "That was you the other night, wasn't it? You do cause a lot of bother."

"Enough, Nelson," the captain barked. He turned to Jessica. "I'm afraid I have no choice. Give me the ring right now, or you're spending the night in jail."

Jessica wept as the handcuffs closed around her wrists. "But I didn't take anything," she sobbed. "Somebody get my sister. I didn't take that ring."

As the Juma police officers led her down the gangplank, a single ray of hope penetrated the gloom.

She was in trouble again, big trouble, which meant that her mystery man might appear and swoop her off to safety.

She searched the shadows in vain. No one came to her rescue.

Groaning, Denise stowed the paddle. "Rub my back, Win," she gasped. "I overdid it at the gym today."

Winston tenderly massaged the knotted muscles at the base of her neck. "What I don't understand is why you're still talking to me."

"No offense, Winston, but who else is there to talk to at the moment?"

226

"Even so, ninety-nine out of a hundred women would be telling me what a supreme jerk I am," Winston persisted. "If they were telling me anything at all."

Denise reached over her shoulders to hold his hands. "Is that ninety-nine by actual count?" she asked lightly.

He smiled, even though she had her back to him. "Be honest. Don't you get fed up with me sometimes? Don't you wish I were, you know, more masterful? I mean, here we are, in a very small boat on a very big sea, and I'm pretty much useless. No folding fishing rod in my backpack, no dehydrated water in my pocket . . . I don't even have a Swiss army knife. What good am I?"

"You're very decorative," Denise said, turning around to drink in the lovable face. "And you've done half the paddling."

"Okay, okay," Winston said, "I can take a hint. It's my turn again. But let's just sit here watching the sky for a minute." He kissed the top of her head. "I have to admit it, Denise. I'm a teensy bit—um, perturbed. How about you? Underneath that calm facade—"

"Lurks a heart pounding madly. But it's a sort of calm madness," she added. "Do you know what I mean?"

He dropped more kisses into her hair. Even

after a day of being spritzed by salt, her hair still smelled wonderful.

"Actually I do know what you mean," he said. "Like, we really might not make it to land, but here we are with each other, so it's the worst and best of all possible worlds."

"Exactly," she said.

They held each other without talking for a while, listening to the sound of the waves hitting the tiny boat.

"If I die and you don't—" Winston began.

"Shhh," she said. "Nobody's going to die. Dying's not our sort of thing, Winnie."

"If I die," he repeated firmly, "I want you to make a promise. Cross your heart and swear that someday you'll name a son Winston."

"Are you serious?"

"Deadly," he said. "If you'll excuse the expression. Winston Egbert whatever."

"Winston Egbert Whatever," she repeated. "It has a certain ring."

"Well, not literally 'whatever.' Winston Egbert—"

"Nelson," she supplied helpfully. "Winston Egbert Nelson."

"Nelson! Are you crazy? Bryan would never agree to name a child after me! Anyway, I can't see you two together at all. I mean, the guy's about as much fun as breakfast on Pleasure Island."

"Well, I guess that leaves the charming Bruce Patman, then."

"Denise, are you nuts? Winston Egbert Patman?" He bit his lip. "I didn't know you had such terrible taste in men. It makes me a little bit worried about myself."

She laughed tenderly. "Don't be," she said. "I was just trying to frighten you. Into staying alive."

"Whew! You're sure?"

"Oh, yeah."

"Well, I guess your terror tactic worked," he said, reaching for the paddle. "Because I'm getting my second wind."

The light in the sky started fading so fast, it was as if it were controlled by a dimmer. Reaching as far as he could, pulling as hard as he could, Winston paddled for all he was worth.

"Juma, here we come!" he shouted.

At last he felt like a man worthy of Denise.

"I think I can!" he crowed. "I think I can, I think I can, I—oops."

For a long moment, Denise didn't say anything. "Winston, did you say 'oops'?"

"I don't think you want to know." Winston's voice was the merest whisper.

"Oops, as in—"

He sighed heavily. "I dropped the paddle."

Denise was quiet for almost a full minute.

"Well, look at it this way. At least that leaves your arms free. In case you'd like to hold me."

Numbly, he put his arms around Denise and pulled her very close. "I love you, Denise."

"I love you too, Win," she answered.

There was nothing more to say.

Darkness descended around them. "Help!" Winston croaked into the vast nothingness. "Help!"

Are Winston and Denise ever going to see the gang from SVU again? Or will the ocean become their watery grave? Find out in Sweet Valley University 14, **SHIPBOARD WEDDING**.

We hope you enjoyed reading this book. If you would like to receive further information about available titles in the Bantam series, just write to the following address, with your name and address:

Kim Prior
Bantam Books
61–63 Uxbridge Road
London W5 5SA.

If you live in Australia or New Zealand and would like more information about the series, please write to:

Sally Porter
Transworld Publishers
(Australia) Pty Ltd
15–25 Helles Avenue
Moorebank
NSW 2170
AUSTRALIA

Kiri Martin
Transworld Publishers (NZ) Ltd
3 William Pickering Drive
Albany
Auckland
NEW ZEALAND

SWEET VALLEY HIGH™

The top-selling teenage series starring identical twins Jessica and
Elizabeth Wakefield and all their friends at Sweet Valley High.

A great new series from Bantam Books . . .

Nobody Forgets Their First Love!

Now there's a romance series that gets to the heart of *everyone's* feelings about falling in love. *Love Stories* reveals how boys feel about being in love, too! In every story, a boy and girl experience the real-life ups and downs of being a couple, and share in the thrills, joys, and sorrows of first love.

Coming soon from Bantam Books:

1. MY FIRST LOVE *by Callie West*
2. SHARING SAM *by Katherine Applegate*
3. HOW TO KISS A GUY *by Elizabeth Bernard*
4. THE BOY NEXT DOOR *by Janet Quin-Harkin*